Owned by the Billionaire

J.L. Ryan

Published by J.L. Ryan, 2018.

This is a work of fiction. Similarities to real people, places, or events are entirely coincidental.

OWNED BY THE BILLIONAIRE

First edition. June 1, 2018.

ISBN: 978-1393297963

Written by J.L. Ryan.

The Billionaire's Gift

April's mind still reeled from the news. It was all anyone in her sorority house talked about, and all that she saw on the news. Lewis Edwards had been arrested and charged with securities fraud. It turned out that the investment scheme he was running truly was a scheme – a Ponzi scheme. He was bringing in new investors, most of them hardworking middle class looking to build retirement funds, and using the money to pay his high net worth investors. It all came crashing down on him, and in an attempt to pay back as much of the money as they could, the Feds seized all of Edwards' assets.

The problem for April was that Lewis Edwards was her father.

April would never have considered herself rich, but she was wealthy. They had enough money that she never worried about anything. She never even questioned why her mother left her father five years ago – though she suspected now that her mother got wise to his scheme and decided to leave. April felt badly now for insisting to stay with him. She had alienated her mother, and right now, she could have used a sympathetic shoulder to cry on.

Everyone had abandoned her. Her boyfriend of two years broke up with her. Her friends turned their backs on her. April was alone and miserable. As the spring semester wrapped up, April somehow managed to make it through her finals and wondered what would happen next. Would she be able to come back to school? Would she even have a place to live? The home she had known her whole life was locked up and taped. It and everything inside was to be auctioned off this summer.

April sat on the bed of her dorm room and looked out the window. Her roommate Sylvia had already left. Sylvia had hardly said a word to her since the news about her father came out. Of all of her friends, April thought Sylvia had the best reason. Her father had been one of the investors in the Edwards Fund, and he very likely lost a great deal of money.

The day outside was bright, far brighter than April felt. She let out a long sigh. She had held off on calling her mother. She knew that her mother would not turn her away, but she was also not sure how she was going to get to her. She was across the country now, in California. While she had managed to pick up her life, April doubted that she would be able to spring for a plane ticket at the last minute.

"You're still here," a light voice said from April's doorway.

April turned to see her sorority sister Chloe standing there. She was holding a suitcase in one hand and a box under her other arm.

"Yeah, I'm not in any hurry to get nowhere," April said.

Chloe set her things down at the doorway and walked over to Sylvia's old bed. She sat down and looked at April, measuring her carefully. April was not sure what to make of it. She and Chloe were never close. Chloe was a year her senior and a sweet girl, but the two of them had almost nothing in common.

"It's been hard on you the last few weeks," Chloe said at last. "Do you know where you're going?"

April shrugged her shoulders. "I'll probably call my mom out in California and see if I can join her out there."

Chloe frowned. "That's a long way to go for an 'if you can.'"

April appreciated Chloe's ability to quickly understand a situation; even she did not understand all of the details behind it. It did not help her though, and April let out another deep sigh before looking out the window again.

"You know," Chloe said, "I might have a solution for you."

April turned back to face Chloe. A solution was just what she needed. "What's that?"

"My dad owns a resort upstate. He always needs extra help for the summer, and it pays really well. You also get to stay at the resort free, though you're staying in the servants quarters. It's not too bad, as long as you don't mind spending your summer in a room about the size of this dorm room."

April never had to work a summer job. She was aware of the concept, but the practice itself was alien to her. Still, the idea of getting a job had a certain appeal. It meant that she did not have to depend on her mother, and if her mother saw her trying to make an effort to get past everything and be better for it, it might help the two of them repair their relationship. If her mother could help, she might even be willing to do it on more even terms than April having to move somewhere strange.

"Will it be a problem, to get me a job I mean?" April asked.

Chloe shook her head. "My dad's opinion is that anyone who can't ask a few simple questions about an investment probably deserves to lose their money." Chloe paused and gave April an apologetic look. "It's a harsh opinion. But it means that he's not going to have anything against helping you. Besides, nothing that happened had anything to do with you. It was all your father."

April gave Chloe the first real smile that she felt in weeks. "Thank you so much. Whatever he needs me to do, I don't care. I'll even wash toilets."

Chloe laughed. "It won't be that bad. It'll be hard work, but the resort is beautiful, and staff always get two days off during the week, so you'll even get to enjoy some of it."

April did not care about getting to enjoy the resort. For the first time since the investigation into her father started, April was starting to see the light at the end of a very dark tunnel.

She even thought it might not be a train.

****

April had never had the opportunity to visit Stuart Estates before. It was far more upscale than anything her family would have afforded, though she knew many of her father's clients probably frequented this resort. She wished she had gotten to see and enjoy it without having to be an employee. Set in a mountain valley, it featured a large manor house that hosted any number of events, from conferences to weddings and family reunions. Some of the upstairs rooms were still held as private rooms for guests, though a majority of guest accommodations were in "cabins," buildings that had once served as guest houses or were built later when the original property was converted.

Still, April thought that she would enjoy working here. The air was crisp and clear. She was surrounded by beauty. It was tranquil, even if her supervisor Henry Graven did promise that she would be far too busy to take notice of what was around them.

Mr. Graven was a cold man, tall with pale skin and dark hair. April recognized the name right away, and did her best not to cringe. He was one of the people who lost their retirement money to her father's scheme. She could tell by the way that he looked at her; he knew who she was. He would not be able to do anything overt, but if she gave him any reason to fire her, he would not hesitate to take it.

Her first day was mostly a learning curve, of going from being the person waited on to doing the waiting. Mr. Graven was grudgingly patient as she learned, and she found the rest of the staff to be kind and understanding. She did not think any of them knew about her circumstances, and she was thankful for that. It was still a stressful day, and she was happy to retire in the evening to her room.

Her "room" was one-half of a small cabin that April thought had probably been a campground cabin at some point. Now it was fitted with lighting and a small window unit to control heat and air. A bathroom had also been built onto it, to be shared between the two units. It was small, smaller than her dorm room had been, but it was comfortable, brightly decorated, and most of all private.

April lay on her bed and thought about her day. It has been busy. Mr. Graven was right. She had barely had time to notice the beautiful scenery around her. She decided she would change that. She would give herself a few days to get used to the job, and after that, she would take brief moments in her day to just appreciate where she was.

****

April knelt down to wipe up the spilled coffee and gather up the shards of china cups that were now scattered about the floor. She was still getting used to carrying trays and keeping them balanced. Something had brushed her thigh over her skirt – it was not a something, it was a man's hand, she was certain of that – and caused her to lose her balance. Now, she was mortified as guests watched her fumbling with the glass shards and spilt coffee, trying hard not to cut herself.

When the last piece was gathered and the last of the coffee sopped up, April stood, careful not to tip her tray and spill any of the shards. As she walked past a table, she felt a hand brush the top of her knee. She glanced back to see an older man with short, thick grey hair give her a wink. She quickly turned, trying to control her blush and pushed through the swinging doors back into the kitchen galley.

"Are you okay?" Leah, one of the other girls on staff asked her as she set down her tray of broken cups.

"A guest is getting grabby," April said. She let out a sigh as she began to move the shards into the collection bin set up for broken wares. "It just caught me off guard, that's all."

"You should be more careful with your tray Miss Edwards." Mr. Graven paused as he walked past her. "You are lucky that you did not burn anyone."

"I'm sorry. I'll be more careful next time," April said.

She did not look up to see Mr. Graven's look, but she was sure it was one of contempt. He walked on and she finished depositing the shards and took her tray to be washed. Another tray of coffee was set up, which Leah picked up to take out. April was relieved. She did not want to have to go back out into the dining room right now, not right on the heels of something so embarrassing.

The rest of the noon day brunch went by smoothly, and when April did have to go back out, she was glad to see that guests paid her no more attention than they did to any other member of staff. Slowly the guests filed out of the dining hall and out to the veranda. It was still raining lightly outside, but it would clear soon. The guests would enjoy any number of outdoor festivities while the staff prepared the indoor rooms for evening festivities.

April moved to her area of the dining room and began cleaning the tables. Someone else would come behind to vacuum, but she wanted to make sure that the floor was cleared of any large debris. As with everything else, she was still getting accustomed to cleaning, and the rest of the staff were done and cleared away as she still worked, her mind turning over bits of half-remembered lyrics to keep her moving at a steady pace.

A hand moved over the small of April's back and along her buttock. She jumped up, pushing into the bulk of someone behind her. April had not even heard anyone come up on her. When she turned, she saw the same man with the grabby hands from brunch.

"You're like a little rabbit." His voice was smooth as he spoke. His eyes were even and demanding. April gripped the table and tried to put space between them, only to have him close it again. "I do like hunting rabbits."

"I need to finish my work." April could not think of anything else to say. The man's hands moved to her waist and slowly up her sides to cup her breasts.

Everything happened at once then. The swinging door from the kitchen galley opened. Mr. Graven walked out, followed by two other staff members. The door from the veranda opened and an older woman walked in, followed by two young men. April's hand collided with the face of the man accosting her with a loud slap propelled by the swing of her arm. It resounded through the dining hall before the woman began to scream shrilly.

April tried to wrestle control of her situation, but she could not. Mr. Graven was upon the scene immediately, asking the man – Henry Worthington as it turned out to April's surprise and horror – if he were okay. The woman screamed about a trollop hitting her husband. Mr. Worthington began his explanation of how she had come onto him. April tried to speak up, to give her side of the story, only to be hushed by Mr. Graven or Mrs. Worthington screaming about lies. The noise brought more guests from the veranda into the dining room.

Mr. Graven finally took hold of April's arm, squeezing tightly and leading her away. She tried to protest over his assurances to Mr. Worthington that he would take care of the situation. He led her out into the hall and spun her around hard, slamming her back against the wall and knocking the air from her. Further down, guests poured out of the dining room and into the hall, not wanting to miss the end of the drama.

"I have been very patient with you, but I will not have you accosting our guests," Mr. Graven kept his voice stern and even.

"I didn't do anything wrong," April said.

"You slapped one of the resorts most honored guests. You will go up to him and you will apologize."

"I will not. The man is a pig!" April said louder than she meant to.

Mr. Graven pulled back his hand and aware of the crowd stopped himself. He lowered his voice and leaned in closer to April. "You are fired, do you understand? You will go to your cabin and pack your belongings. I expect to see you gone from here within the hour."

April could not say anything else. She turned and ran down the hall as tears began to stream from her eyes, burning her cheeks in her shame and embarrassment.

****

Nigel Conroy knew two things very well. Henry Worthington was a misogynist and a womanizer and the staff of Stuart would happily kiss the ground that he walked on. He was certain that Worthington could have murdered the poor girl and the staff supervisor would still have found a way to claim she had fallen upon his knife or gun herself.

He also had a very good idea of who the girl was. He face was familiar, one he knew he had seen recently on the news. If he was right, she had been through enough. Being fired in front of all of the guests here was the last thing she needed. As the crowd began to slowly disperse, he took hold of the arm of another staff, a cute young woman with short blonde hair.

"I'm sorry, but I wanted to ask you something before you had a chance to go away," Nigel said, releasing her.

"It's alright sir," the young woman said. "How can I help you?"

"The girl that just ran down the hall, what was her name?"

The young woman narrowed her eyes, and Nigel did not blame her. He sensed protectiveness and found himself very much liking this young woman.

"I don't mean any harm, but she didn't deserve what happened, and I think you know it. I'm pretty sure I've seen you here for a few seasons, so I think you know what really happened. I just want to make sure she'll be okay."

The young woman continued to eye him warily. Nigel did his best to project his sincerity and she finally relaxed. "April Edwards. I can take you to see her. We share the same cabin."

Nigel nodded his head. "Thank you. If anyone says anything, just tell them I pulled you aside to help me with an errand. I'll vouch for you, I promise."

The young woman did not say anything else. She simply turned and Nigel understood he was expected to follow her. She led him through a side door of the main estate house. The morning rain was now stopped, and the humidity of the afternoon was quickly setting in. She kept a brisk pace as she led him to the servant's cabins and to what he presumed to be her own.

Nigel stepped in to a small living area with a couch, chair, and television and three doors that along the two adjacent and one opposite walls.

The young woman turned to the left door and knocked gently. "April sweetie, it's Leah."

"Please go away, Leah. I don't want to talk to anyone," April's muffled voice came through the door, thick with her tears.

Leah looked back at Nigel but he nodded, waving his hand to urge her to continue.

"April, there's a man here to see you," Leah said.

The door swung open and April appeared, her face streaked with tears and fire in her eyes. Nigel felt a great deal of respect for her suddenly, and felt very badly for anyone that earned that ire. He thought she could have a fiery temper, one she might not even be aware of.

"I'll gouge out that bastard's eyes if it's him," April said before her eyes had a chance to survey the room. When they fell on Nigel, some of the fire pulled back, though he noticed it did not withdraw completely. "Who is that?"

"He's one of the guests," Leah said. "He wanted to make sure you were okay."

April stood there and studied Nigel before turning back to her friend. "Tell him I'll be fine."

"Can I speak to you for a few minutes?" Nigel took a step forward.

Leah looked from Nigel to April, and he could see the helplessness in her eyes. She had duties to attend to and could not be playing referee between them.

April sighed and placed a hand on Leah's shoulder. "It's fine. You get back up before you get into trouble too."

Leah hesitated, looked between the two of them again. She finally nodded. "You find me before you go, okay?"

"I will. Thank you." April gave Leah a hug. She released her and Leah walked past Nigel, giving him a careful look that he read very well. April had a bad enough day, and he did not need to make it worse.

As Leah walked out of the cabin, Nigel turned his attention to the young woman before him as she stepped out of her room. She wore only the simple black dress common to all of the staff. The white apron had been discarded somewhere, either in her room or thrown aside as she fled the shameful scene.

"You have a good friend. Have the two of you known each other a long time?" Nigel was curious about this young woman. The media had painted her as the aloof princess of a sinister financial king, carefully keeping herself out of the direct light of the media. He was not seeing that here. He was seeing something vastly different.

"Just a few days. Leah is a real gem, though." April tilted her head to one side. "What are you doing here?"

Nigel gave a small laugh. "You're not going to ask who I am?"

April shook her head. "I know who you are. Your face shows up in almost every magazine, usually some story about a broken-hearted girl or a large playboy party."

Nigel brought his hand up to his chest and feigned injury. "You wound me. But that's fair enough. I won't lie. I know who you are too."

April frowned deeply. "Here to gloat then?"

A sharp pain stabbed through Nigel's chest and he was surprised to feel it. He was not sure why he felt so much sympathy for this young woman. She was attractive. Her dark hair and bright, blue eyes would be enough to captivate any man. Something else had drawn him in, however. He just wished that he could put his finger on what it was.

"No," Nigel said simply. "I really did want to make sure you were okay. Do you know what you're going to do?"

April shook her head. "I can't go back down to New York. My face is still all over the television. I guess I get to hope that the few days of pay I have here is enough to fly me out to Los Angeles."

"You don't have anyone that can help you out?" Nigel felt very badly for her now. He knew from the news reports that her father's assets had all been seized. He never imagined that it would leave her destitute. He wondered if anyone had bothered to care about that.

"I talked to my mother. She's working as a waitress and trying to get into acting. She barely has enough money to pay her bills." April paused. "Why am I tell you this?"

Why am I about to do what I'm about to do? Nigel was glad to see that at least both of them were behaving in ways they did not understand. She had an excuse. She was under duress. He had no idea what his excuse was, but he knew he would not be able to stop himself now.

"Would you like to spend the rest of the week here with me, as my guest?" Nigel asked.

April's look of shock made him smile. "What?"

Nigel took in a deep breath and let it out. "I'm not sure why your supervisor was so hard on you, but I'm sure that you did not have it coming. A few broken cups is not worth risking a sexual harassment lawsuit. You don't have anywhere else to go right now. So, take a few days to figure it out. Maybe you and your mother will be able to work out something. In the meantime, enjoy the resort as a guest where your old boss can't touch you. As for Mr. Worthington, have the best revenge you can have on him."

April crossed her arms. "What's that?"

"Show him that it had no ill effect on you. Show him that you're over it and moved on. People who do things like that; they thrive on knowing the chaos they've caused."

Nigel watched April carefully as she considered his proposal. She was wary, and he did not blame her. He knew how quickly people in his own circles could turn if the sensed weakness or unattractive controversy. He did not expect that people in hers would be any different.

She finally uncrossed her arms and gave him a square look, setting her shoulders even. "What's the catch?"

Nigel shook his head. "No catch. You'll have to stay with me, but I have one of the luxury cabins, so you'll have your own room. No expectations, except that you'll accompany me and keep me company. That's all."

April continued to study him carefully. Finally, her stance relaxed. "Okay. I'll accept your invitation."

Nigel nodded. "Good. Do you have street clothes?"

April laughed. "Nothing worthy of a place like this."

"Then I'll add one more caveat to this deal. Allow me to take you into town for a shopping trip."

April nodded. Nigel sat down to wait for her to gather her things. This was a quaint and small cabin. He wondered if she had a chance to see the luxury guest cabins yet, and what she would make of them.

****

April held her shopping bags in her hand as she followed Nigel up the walkway to the large cabin. Large picture windows dominated the façade, glowing through their translucent white shades. He carried her suitcase and occasionally made as though to be bearing too heavy of a weight. She could only laugh at that.

Nigel Conroy the man was nothing like the man in so many magazine articles that she and her sorority sisters would read. She thought he could have his arrogant side, and occasionally as he took her through the shops in town, she saw it, typically, when he put down a dress or outfit because he felt the price tag was too low. Mostly, he was normal, if somewhat impulsive in taking her on as his guest.

He opened the door to the cabin and held it for her to walk in.

It opened immediately to the main room, open with a vaulted ceiling. A large fireplace dominated it with a couch and two oversized chairs set in front of it. A wide high definition television hung above the fireplace and a full entertainment system sat to the left side. Along the left wall stood a bar and to her right the room opened to a dining room and a kitchen. April wondered if it saw use at all and wondered at its inclusion.

A stairway led up in front of her, dividing the mysterious kitchen from the rest of the downstairs. Nigel closed the door behind them and led her up the stairs. To her right another large living area was set up with balcony rails do that it looked down below them. Beyond it was a hall with three doors. Nigel guided her to one and invited her to set down her things. A double bed sat in this room and a elegant dresser. She set her bags down beside the door as Nigel set her suitcase down by the dresser.

"There's a bathroom right across the hall from you. If you don't like this bed, you can try the one in the room next to you. My room is at the end of the hall. I don't know if you do your own laundry. If you do, the French doors in the hall have a small washer and dryer behind them. You can also set your laundry in the bins outside for staff to pick up. It's your choice, but I do my own laundry."

April blinked her eyes. "You do your own laundry?" She tried to imagine this man measuring out detergent and could not imagine it.

"My housekeeper at home taught me after I ruined my own clothes at another resort. I've had bad luck with staff losing my things."

April wondered if his items were lost or taken. Most of the staff here were honest and hardworking, but she supposed that anyone could be tempted to take something that belonged to someone famous. "I suppose you cook too."

Nigel shook his head. "No, that's never a pretty sight. I hoped you did, actually."

April laughed and shook her head. "My cooking is part of our sorority's hazing ritual." She watched as he gave her a dubious look, tilting his head to one side. "I'm serious. I once boiled the coating out of a pan."

Nigel leaned against the doorframe, his look becoming quickly serious and contemplative. "It's not fair, you know."

"I know. I have to be more careful with pots." April wanted the levity. The look in his eyes unsettled her.

"I'm serious. It's fine that the Feds want to make sure your father pays back the money that he's taken. That's good. They can't take away his ability to care for the people he's responsible for. That punishes you for something you didn't do."

April swallowed hard. She did not like the look in Nigel's eyes right now. It made her want to probe and want to understand the depth of empathy that he had in this moment. She did not want to do that. He was being nice to do this for her, but she did not want to complicate things any more than they were already complicated for her.

"Right," Nigel pushed himself from the doorframe. "You've had a busy day, so I'll let you rest. I'll wake you up in the morning and we can go and enjoy brunch and some horseback riding if you like."

"Horseback riding would be nice," April said. "Thank you again."

Nigel smiled as he turned to the hall. "Thank you for accepting my invitation."

****

The young boy stood in front of the blazing fire, his eyes picking up the orange flames, reflecting them back to the world. Tears streamed down his soot-covered face and when he coughed, he sounded congested and full of smoke. Inside, in the flames, was everything he ever knew and understood to be love, compassion, and order. He could not understand what was happening, or why Nana uttered apologies as she tried to clean the soot from his face.

April sat up in bed and took in a deep breath. Vivid dreams did not come on often, but when they did, they always left her feeling strange, as though she were coming back into her own body. It was, she thought, the effect of her mind moving from its dream reality back into the real world.

The dream bothered her, and as her day played back in her mind and she remembered where she was, she understood why.

She had found the story by chance. Her ex-boyfriend had a playboy magazine sitting on his bed, and she flipped through to the life story of Nigel Conroy, as promised on the cover, while he played on his game console. When Nigel was five years old, his mother had set fire to their home. She had drugged her husband and her son's nanny. She spread kerosene through the house, then over herself and her husband, lighting the both of them on fire. As the fire spread, Nigel's cries somehow managed to wake the groggy nanny, who stumbled out of the inferno, holding the crying child.

The image in her dream was an image from the magazine article, a picture that had been taken of the boy as he stood watching the inferno that had been his home. He said in the interview for the article that he did not really remember the day, but it still influenced his life. His mother suffered from mental illness, untreated because both her family and his father had considered the idea of mental illness to be shameful, something that others faced, not them. Nigel had inherited his father's fortune, and when he was old enough to decide a direction for it, created a foundation to encourage the treatment and de-stigmatization of mental illness.

How could she have forgotten such a terrible, tragic story? April put her head in her hands and began crying.

****

April followed Nigel up to the main estate house, where brunch waited for them. She wondered what Mr. Graven would make of her being there, or Leah for that matter. She thought about Chloe, who had gotten her the job to begin with. She hoped that Chloe was not told about what had happened. She hated to think that she would be made to regret helping her.

Brunch was a pleasant affair, full of conversation. They sat at a large table with other resort guests and engaged in polite conversation. A few of the people at her table knew who April was, but none of them seemed to think her situation warranted more than a passing acknowledgement. She was happy for that. She noticed a glare from Mr. Graven. When he attempted to come to the table, Nigel rose and pulled him aside quickly. April did not know what was said exactly, only that it began with, "before you embarrass yourself."

After brunch, they followed the other guests out to the veranda. There was no rain today, and the early afternoon was quickly growing warm. April followed Nigel through the crowd of people as he walked the direction of the stables.

Mr. Worthington backed up, separating her from Nigel and almost causing April to run into him. He turned, startled, and gave her a kindly smile. "My apologies miss. My son was just clowning around as boys are want to do."

"That's okay, Mr. Worthington," April said carefully.

Mr. Worthington blinked his eyes and gave April a broader smile. "Well, I'm afraid you have me at a loss. You know me, but I don't know you."

April smiled, feeling strange and light. After the huge scene the day before, he did not even recognize her face. She supposed that in the world Mr. Worthington inhabited, it was impossible that a woman who was a servant the day before could be a guest today.

She supposed he had never seen Cinderella.

"I'm afraid I'll have to leave it that way," April said. She glided past Mr. Worthington before he could stay anything else. Nigel had stopped and turned. He was now waiting on her, his look quickly becoming confused as she walked up to him.

"What happened?" he asked.

"I just bumped into Mr. Worthington," April said and decided to laugh. "He didn't even recognize me."

Nigel blinked his eyes and tilted his head. April continued on to the steps that led down from the veranda. The stables were ahead, and she wanted to smell the fresh hay and the horses. Mr. Worthington did not think enough of the day to even realize she and the servant he tried to molest were the same person.

If he could not be bothered, she supposed she did not need to either. The thought of putting the incident behind her lightened her step. After weeks of being remembered, a single moment of being forgotten was bliss.

****

Nigel's horse bucked and he pulled up on the reigns to gain control again, watching the young woman who laughed, carefree on the back of her own. She pulled up on the reigns and turned her horse so that she could twist in her saddle to look at him. This time yesterday, she was in tears. Now, she could have been a completely different person. Nigel supposed in a way, she was. All she needed was a glass slipper and they could have been a prince and princess in a fairy tale.

"You shouldn't look so serious," April said. "Horseback riding is supposed to be fun."

"There's fun, and then there's slapping my horse's rump and startling him," Nigel said, but he found her smile to be infectious.

April shrugged her shoulders. "You were riding like an old man. I just wanted to see if you really knew how to ride."

Nigel took in a breath and nodded his head, recognizing the challenge. "I know how to ride, my dear. I took my first lesson at ten years old."

"Seven," April gave him a smug look.

"I still have you on years riding," Nigel said. He was only about six years older than April was, but his pride was wounded now.

They continued their ride along the forest trail and up the mountain. It was beautiful here, and being out here among the natural beauty seemed to have a good effect on April. Nigel was not sure that he understood why her encounter with Mr. Worthington had left her in such a good mood, but it was nice to see that the forest around them was keeping it in place.

They reached the water trough for the horses and dismounted, tying their reigns off on the poles there so the horses could drink and relax. This stop in the ride was along the ridge of the mountain that the horse trail wound. It offered a nice view of the valley and the estate below, and Nigel was happy to see that few others were taking advantage of the stables today. Most were heading out to the cricket grounds or down to the lake.

Nigel turned to look at April, and saw that she was watching him. The look in her eyes was deep and sympathetic. He wondered at it, but was not sure what to ask her. Perhaps she was feeling badly about spooking his horse.

"This is really nice," April said. She turned and looked back over the valley below them. "I really do appreciate you doing this for me."

Nigel stepped up to her and took her hand in his. She did not pull away, and he held it tighter. As they looked over the valley, she talked about horseback riding in the boroughs outside of New York City and spending her entire weekend learning how to care for the horses. It was, she admitted to him, the only chore she ever learned to do, and one that she always loved.

With her face in profile to him, Nigel could see that she was deeper in her thoughts than her words expressed. Was she remembering the good times with her father and mother, or was it just her father? He realized he had no idea how long her mother had been in Los Angeles. It could have been weeks or years. He had the feeling from how she had talked about her prospects of getting there that they two of them were not very close.

April turned to face him, and Nigel found himself caught by her eyes. They were deep and contemplative while bright, catching the sky above them. Nigel brought his hand up to her face, cupping her cheek. He did not think about what he was doing. He simply leaned forward to kiss her.

****

Nigel's kiss was soft and careful, and it moved through April's body quickly, drawing her free hand up to his shoulders. Between her legs, she felt warm and alive. Nigel released her hand and moved his arm around her body, pressing her body closer to him. She could feel him hard against her and her own desire flared, surprising, and delighting her.

He broke away and looked down into her eyes. April wanted his kiss again, and with a flush realized that she wanted more. She imagined their bodies entwined together here along the mountain ridge, where other riders could come upon them at any moment. The idea tingling and warmth between her legs grow and she reached up to kiss him again, finding him responsive and welcoming.

Nigel brought his hand down from her face to her breast and cupped it gently. April wrapped her arms around his neck, running her fingers through Nigel's brown hair and lacing it through her fingers. He squeezed her breast and held her firm against him. April wanted him. She wanted to feel his hands caress her body, to feel him deep inside her. Her body ached and screamed its want, and as the pounding of hooves came up the mountain trail, she could not pull away from him.

They broke their kiss as another pair of riders came up to the trough. April flushed again and looked from Nigel to the newcomers.

"That must be some view," the woman said as she dismounted her horse. She tied it off next to Nigel's own and looked at her partner. "Do you think we can take a look over the ridge too?"

April stifled her laugh and took Nigel's hand, guiding him back to the horses. As they untied theirs from the trough, the new couple moved over to the ridge, sitting on the stone bench. April mounted her horse and waited for Nigel to join her. She considered heading back, but she wanted to push up the mountain. Yes, she wanted Nigel, and she thought if she told him she wanted to go back to his cabin now that he would. She also understood that part of that want came from moments like this, riding together and enjoying each other's company.

She could let it build.

They continued up the mountain trail, passing the new couple as the man put his arm around his companion. April supposed that the view really was romantic. She hoped there would be other such views on their way up.

They rode for another hour, and April could feel the heat of the day working into her body. A stream snaked along the slope of the mountain, coming close to the trail and skirting away from time to time. She thought about the hour, and how nice it would be to have a shower before they went up to the estate house for dinner. When she made the suggestion to Nigel that they head back, he was reluctant at first, until she mentioned showers. The look in his eye brought a new tingle between April's thighs.

As they made their way back down the mountain, they passed the couple that had come up to the water trough. They exchanged waves and continued on, stopping only briefly at the trough to allow the horses to get water. April's mind kept turning to the shower waiting for them, and she did not want to stop any longer than necessary. She thought of water on her skin and Nigel caressing her body and grew impatient to be back.

When they made it back down to the stables, the hands there took the horses from them, removing their tack and rubbing them down gently. They made their way across the estate grounds to the guest cabins, and April looked at Nigel. She could tell that he had something on his mind, and she wanted to be through it before they reached the cabin.

"Is something the matter?" April asked. She could not think of any other way to get conversation starting.

Nigel looked at her and gave her a gentle smile. "It was a beautiful ride, but I'm afraid I was a bit," he paused and looked up to find the words he needed, "presumptuous."

April took in a deep breath and nodded her head. Oh, to get him to see how much she wanted that kiss. She did not want to come across as someone easy, or who was trying to get something from him, but she knew exactly what she wanted from the rest of her evening.

"I told you I wasn't going to make any demands, and here I am crossing that line." Nigel placed his hands in his pockets. "It's not fair to you."

April twisted up her lips in thought and nodded again. "It's not." When he snapped his head to her, she gave him a smile. "Well, it wouldn't be if I weren't receptive to it."

Nigel narrowed his eyes and gave her a smile. He took her hand and picked up his pace. When they reached his cabin, he opened the door and she walked inside. When he closed the door behind them, his arms were around her body, pulling her back against him. April sighed and eased her stance so that she could feel his hardness pressing against her.

"I want you so badly I can taste it," Nigel whispered into her ear. He nibbled the lobe gently.

April turned around in his arms and brought her hands up to his shoulders. He pulled her tighter against him and April rose up to kiss him again. His tongue moved between her lips and danced with hers. She could taste his desire in his breath and wanted to drown in it. She brought her hands around to the collar of his shirt and slowly worked her way down his buttons.

When he broke the kiss, Nigel lifted April's shirt above her head, discarding it to the side and shedding his own. He moved his hands down to her waist and unbuttoned her shorts, pushing them down her body. He started to kneel, and a panic filled April.

"I'm sweaty from the ride," April said. She wanted what his kneeling offered, but she wanted it to be perfect.

Nigel stood. "Then let's have that shower."

He pushed down her shorts and underwear in one motion. April slipped out of her shoes and her clothing, releasing the catch of her bra behind her back and dropping that as well. She was naked before Nigel, and as his eyes took in her body, she shuddered, nervous. Would he find her pleasing?

"You are beautiful." Nigel placed his hands at her waist and pulled her to him again. He kissed her deeply and then released her, gesturing her to walk up the stairs. He guided her back to his bedroom with its oversized king bed dominating the room, and then to the bathroom beyond.

A large garden tub stood at one end of the bathroom. Next to it was a double size shower with stone tiling. April stepped up to it, and twisted the knobs on either side to start the water. Nigel stepped up behind her and she could feel him, naked now, pressing against her. She stepped into the shower and he followed.

Nigel took a large sponge and poured soap on it, lathering it in the stream of water that sprinkled over them. He brought it to April's body and caressed, leaving the soapy lather behind to be quickly washed away by the water. He moved along her chest, her arms, and her torso before moving down between and down her legs. When he finished, his lips were there, at her sex taking it in. April gasped and pressed her hands to the wall to support herself. His mouth was magic there, drawing her desire out of her and building it into a wave to crash over her body. She shivered as her body counted every bead of water that struck her.

When he stood, April took the sponge from him, lathering it again, and running it across his shoulders, down his torso, and up his back. She brought it down to clean his manhood carefully and knelt, kissing what was now clean and hard softly before washing his legs, stroking down and then up along them gently. When she was through, she wanted to take him into her mouth, but he took hold of her arms and pulled her up. He kissed her and brought her leg up, pressing himself between her thighs.

She welcomed the feel of him hard and firm as he penetrated her. April wanted to feel him deeper, and when he brought her other leg up, she wrapped them around his body. He held her thighs and trust deeper into her and she felt alive and desirous. She kissed him passionately as he pressed her against the wall, seeking the depth of her, joining with her in their shared passion. When he pulsed into her, April took hold of his hair, gripping it between her fingers, reveling as he pushed still deeper into her.

When he was spent, he lowered her legs gently. April found them wobbly and weak, and stood under the warmth of the water, letting it pour energy back into them. Nigel kissed her again and pulled away, smiling as he dipped his head under the stream of water to wash his hair.

"I like showers," April said. She brought her own head under the showerhead and hoped that the water would mask her embarrassment over saying something so silly.

Nigel looked at her. "They can be very nice, when the company is."

A playfulness moved through April and she tilted her head to one side as she reached for shampoo. "I tried to be very nice and you stopped me."

Nigel laughed. "I didn't think that good girls were supposed to do that."

April's mind turned and spun at his teasing. "I'm in a shower with a man I just met yesterday. How good of a girl can I be?"

April's breath caught at the look in Nigel's eyes. It was both dark and desirous, and empathetic and sincere. She had no way to respond to it, and no word for the feeling it drew up inside her. She wanted to throw her arms around him and run away screaming at the same time. Overcome by her fear and desire, she could only stand there, her hands at her head, ready to massage shampoo into her scalp.

"You can be as good as you want to be," Nigel said.

He brought shampoo up to his own head and closed his eyes as he worked it through his hair. April swallowed hard and washed her own as well. When he opened his eyes again, the depth of emotion had passed. April suppressed a shiver and wondered once again at this man. He was a playboy. This week and this affair was one of many he had, one of many that he would have.

Some small part of her mind tried to challenge that, and April quashed it quickly as she rinsed her hair and turned off her side of the shower.

This was just an affair, just like any other Nigel Conroy had. He was taking a young woman he saw in distress and helping her through it the only way he knew how to. She bore him no ill will for that. In fact, April thought the world could use a few more Nigels.

****

The dining hall was lit brightly tonight, and a string quartet played Vivaldi as guests entered. Nigel led April to a table for two and they sat down, waiting patiently for a server to come by. Evening meals were meant to be more intimate, but the menu was still a general fare for all guests, a choice of steak, chicken, or fish, with either rice or potatoes and summer vegetables. April decided that she would have the fish and rice while Nigel ordered a steak and requested a bottle of wine to be brought out to them.

April spotted Leah among the servers and gave her a small wave. She did not want to embarrass Nigel, and while she thought he would understand her wanting to say hello to her friend, she knew that the other guests would consider the gesture to be gauche at best. Leah gave her a small and excited wave, looking from April to Nigel and back. She mouthed, "wow" as she poured water for another table, and moved to another. April gave an innocent shrug and smiled.

Nigel looked over his shoulder and back to April, smiling. "I think you've inspired new dreams in the female staff."

April laughed. "If only it were that easy for romance." She paused and thought about her last two days. "I'm not even sure how this happened."

Nigel reached under the table and brushed April's knee lightly. She could see he wanted to say something, but before he could, a man walked up to the table. Nigel withdrew his hand casually and looked up at the newcomer.

It took April a moment to register who the man was, and panic filled her. This was Chloe's father, and she could imagine the story told to him, and the reprimand her friend received. April had never met Michael Stuart, when she was hired on, she only worked with Mr. Graven, but she understood him to be a shrewd and clever businessman.

"Mr. Conroy, it is always a pleasure to have you here at the Estate." Mr. Stuart turned his attention to April and gave her a broad smile. "Ms. Edwards, it is good to see that you're enjoying your stay with Mr. Conroy. My daughter sends her regards."

April relaxed at the tone in Mr. Stuart's voice. Whatever story had gotten to his ears, it was either not believed, or countered, perhaps by Chloe herself. April made a note to herself. If she could not find her friend this summer, she would do so during the school year – assuming she was able to get back down to New York City to attend the university. "Thank you. Please tell Chloe I said hello."

Mr. Stuart nodded his head. "I will. She's enjoying a nice trip in Europe right now. She's spending the summer studying there as part of a fellowship. I will be sure to let her know when I talk to her. The both of you enjoy your evening."

He walked away from the table and over to another. April looked to Nigel to see him smiling wisely.

"What?" she asked.

"You looked like a deer caught in headlights for a moment there," Nigel said.

"The whole reason that I had a job here is because Chloe convinced her father to hire me. I was afraid that the worst of what happened reached him."

Nigel shook his head. The server brought their wine and poured a glass for each of them. When she left, leaving the bottle on the table between them, Nigel spoke. "I doubt anyone would have dared saying anything to him. The whole situation would have had him asking too many questions and probably getting other people not you fired. He probably wouldn't do anything to Worthington, though he should, but there are limits to what even Mr. Stuart can do."

April sipped her wine. She had not thought about just how precarious of a position that Mr. Graven really was in with how he had fired her and why. It occurred to her that she could file a complaint, but she realized she did not want to. Mr. Graven seemed to really care about his staff. His attitude toward her did not mask that. She doubted the scene would have played out quite the same way if it had been anyone else. The situation may have been hushed. The girl may even have been reassigned to other duties while Mr. Worthington was here. She thought that other things aggravated the situation, and while it was not right for Mr. Graven to hold her accountable for her father's actions; it was not worth him losing his job over.

"You're a good person," Nigel said.

April blushed, wondering if he read her mind, or if he just understood the situation itself. "Thank you."

"I mean it, you are." Nigel sipped his wine. "Anyway, I'm glad that you accepted my invitation."

"I am too."

They enjoyed their dinner together, using time to chat and get to know each other a little better. That tiny voice April's head tried to ask her if that was the kind of conversation that playboys engaged in, and she refused to answer. Her life was complicated, very complicated. She did not need to complicate someone else's as well.

After dinner, they wandered the estate house, seeing what festivities were taking place tonight. A company was holding an important shareholder meeting in one of the conference rooms. Both of them thought that was too boring to enjoy. Staff cleared the dining hall and the string quartet continued playing music. Guests who were not taking part in the shareholder meeting or any of the other smaller events filled up the dining hall, dancing to baroque music and enjoying the evening on the veranda.

April and Nigel joined in this. Nigel showed April a few simple steps for ballroom dancing, and they moved together to the music. With his arm around her waist, leading her in steps, April felt her desire swell up through her body again. She wanted to kiss him and knew that would not be proper here. They spotted the couple from the trail and exchanged smiles. As they danced past, April caught a snippet of their conversation and realized they were enjoying their anniversary here together.

"This is a magical place," April said as Nigel guided her off the dancefloor and over to a table where drinks were set out for guests.

"Oh?" Nigel handed her a glass of punch and looked at her curiously.

"The couple on the trail today, they're enjoying their anniversary here."

Nigel glanced out to the floor. "Is that so?"

"Apparently. I wonder how many other people are here for special occasions."

Nigel paused as he brought his glass to his lips and considered the people out on the dance floor. "I've never thought about it. I always just come up here and enjoy the mountains and the lake. I don't really think about what is going on with the rest of the guests unless I know them personally."

"I wonder about people sometimes," April said. "When I was a child, I would watch people on the street and wonder where they were going to and coming from. When we would be in a restaurant, I would imagine what conversations people were having at other tables. I always found my life to be easy and boring, so it was a fun way to make things interesting."

"Oh for things to be easy and boring."

April looked and saw Nigel's eyes turn dark with thought again. She supposed that for him, a boring life would have been ideal. She could not imagine what it would have been like for him. Did he have grandparents battle for custody of him, or did servants and lawyers raise him. He did not talk about that in the Playboy interview. April found herself curious again, and wondered if she would have the chance to explore that deep into him.

They danced for a few more songs before walking out onto the veranda and back up to Nigel's cabin. They held hands as they walked, taking in the view of the stars above them. April concentrated on trying to remember the names of any of the stars and constellations she saw and was ashamed that she could not. She should know them. She had learned about them in high school.

She never applied herself, and that knowledge drove home her precarious situation. She always assumed that he father's money would be there to take care of her. She would just move from that security to the security of a man. Now, that option was not open to her. She was not marriageable material. She was fine for a fling, but she did not want to live her life being the naughty fling of rich men.

She was going to have to decide on a direction for herself. She realized that depending on her mother was not the answer either. She was an adult. It was time that she acted it, and took on the responsibilities that brought.

Nigel let her into the cabin and followed her inside. He walked to the fireplace and turned on the gas starter. The logs, April realized, were only for show, to create a simulated fireplace. It was still beautiful, however, and she found herself pushing aside her thoughts and worries for another day.

She walked over to the couch and sat down. Nigel joined her and when he leaned close to her, April welcomed his kiss and his arms around her waist. She thought of making love to him in front of the fireplace and her excitement grew.

He broke the kiss and brought his hand up to April's cheek. She looked into Nigel's eyes and wondered at what thoughts were behind them. His eyes still looked contemplative and serious.

"I want you to stay with me," Nigel said.

April smiled. "I can sleep in your room if you'd like." She knew that was not what he meant, even as she said the words. She did not want to have the conversation that was coming. She realized that she had been running from it since their shower today and she thought she understood why now.

"That will be nice, but that's not what I mean," Nigel said.

April put her finger on his lips. He took her hand and kissed the back of it, bringing it back down to her lap.

"It is not fair," he said. "You're going through something you should not have to go through. Nothing that happened is your fault, but you're suffering for it."

"Lots of people suffer for things that aren't there fault." April suspected that Nigel suffered a lot. What was it actually like, growing up the son of a woman who killed herself and her husband? How many years did he spend wondering if that would happen to him? How many people treated him as if it would?

Nigel let out a sigh. "They do. I would help every single one of them if I could. We can't. We can only help those we can." He paused and sat back. "Do you know about what happened when I was a child?"

April nodded her head. "I read an interview where you talked some about it."

"The woman who took me out of the fire, she was my nanny. She was a kind woman. She was stern, and I grew up thinking she was mean sometimes. She took care of me. She did not have to stay with me. She could have let my family's lawyers find someone else. She was burned very badly in the fire. I lied when I told the interviewer I didn't remember the night very well. I did, but I didn't want to talk about it. She refused to let the paramedics treat her or take her to the hospital until she knew I was okay. She ended up being scarred very badly because of that, but it was the kind of woman she was. She stayed because I was the person she could help."

April took in a deep breath and squeezed Nigel's hand tightly.

"I want to help you. You were not working here because you wanted to. You were here because you had to be. No one should have to work like that. I don't want you to have to work like that."

April felt her heart filling and breaking at the same time. She cared about Nigel, more deeply and more quickly than she thought she would ever care about anyone. She could see herself easily falling in love with him, if she were not there already. She appreciated what he wanted to do, and she thought she understood what it meant to him.

That did not mean she could just accept it.

"Did you know I couldn't name a single constellation in the sky tonight?" April asked.

Nigel gave a small laugh. "I think I know the Big Dipper and Little Dipper. Not everyone knows the constellations."

"No, but people can point to the things they do know," April said. "I can't. My whole life I have depending on other people. I depended on my father to put me through school. I knew I just had to wait to get married and have another man to depend on for my livelihood. If it didn't work out, I would be able to get a nice alimony settlement and probably more money from Daddy again.

"I can't do that anymore. It doesn't matter that it's not fair. It matters that it life now. If I go back to school, I can get a real degree. I can figure out what I want to do with my life and do it, and not have to depend on anyone else."

Nigel brought his hand up to her cheek again. "It's a hard place, I know. The most important person in your life let you down, and depending on another person after that is scary. What happens if I let you down?"

April felt her heart break. She did not want to look at Nigel that way, but he was right. That was exactly what she was scared of. It was more than that, though. She could not expect him to pick up where others left off in taking care of her. It was not just a matter of what he might do anymore. It was what she had to do.

"You're such a wonderful person," April said. She leaned against the back cushion of the couch and let herself gaze into Nigel's eyes. "From most of the stories I've read about you, you're this carefree playboy who does philanthropy and just enjoys his money. You really are so much more than that. It's not that I think you would hurt me. I'm scared of it, but I know better. It's also what I have to do for me."

Nigel leaned his head against the back cushion and looked at her, silent in whatever contemplation he was in.

"I have no idea how I'm going to do this. A lot of people work their way through college. Some of them take student loans. I can do that too if I have to. If I talk to the financial counselors, they'll help me find a job and work out a schedule that I can pay for. I can always change schools if I need to. People do it every day. I'm no one special; I just thought I was for a long time."

Nigel let out a deep breath. She could see understanding and acceptance in his eyes.

"I could see you with a career. I think if you find something that you're passionate about, you could really put yourself into it and do something amazing," he said. "I would like to see that."

April smiled. "Thank you."

"Can I pay for school?" Nigel sat up again.

April was stunned and unsure how to answer his question. He had turned this around somehow and she felt as though she had been flipped on her head. "Pay for school?"

Nigel nodded. "I see the people who work their way through college. Sometimes they can pursue what they want. Sometimes they have to compromise. I want you to find and pursue whatever you want. I can pay for your school. You can stay on campus or with me, which ever you want. I won't pressure you there, though I would like to keep seeing you after this week."

April's mind was still trying to catch up to this strange change in their conversation. She tried to find words, and could not get anything to make sense from her mind to her mouth.

"You can say yes," Nigel said. "I would really like that."

April let out a laugh and sat up. She shook her head and looked down, trying to let her mind finish playing catch up. Nigel was serious about helping her. She did not think it was just some passing fancy of his. His understanding and his persistence told her how intent he was on this. She looked up and smiled at him. "Okay. But I get to pay you back for my school, even if I'm just donating it to your foundation. I appreciate it, but I want to be able to give something back to you."

Nigel returned her smile and broadened it. "I can accept that. You will have to apply yourself, though. I fully expect you to find a career that you can follow through on."

April moved closer to him on the couch. "I promise. I'll think about it this summer and decide." She paused before kissing him and pulled back. "What do I do during the summers?"

Nigel put his arms around her waist and pulled her down to him. "I'm sure we can negotiate something."

He kissed her. April welcomed his tongue through her lips. She thought again of making love to him in front of the fireplace and moved her hands up to unbutton his shirt.

It was a good place to start.

The Billionaire's Game

Sierra stared at her reflection and sighed heavily. Her hair, always tightly drawn up in a ponytail, gave the impression that she had a very angular face. She turned her head from side-to-side, looking at all of the planes that made up who she was. Her hair was a copper brown and her eyes blue. She had a smattering of freckles across her nose and cheeks that gave her a playful look. She had full lips that were always tinted as though she were drinking Kool-Aid, never forcing her to wear lipstick to give herself some more color.

Not that she ever wore make-up, really. As a waitress, she rarely had the time to care about things like make- up, or much else for that matter. She sat there contemplating what she could do to make herself pretty, or what she could do to improve her looks, or at the very least, make her more exotic or something.

She should have never agreed to stand in for Katie on a blind date. It's not so much that she was going to stand in for Katie on the date, it was that she had to actually pretend that she was Katie. It was just as much her own fault for saying yes, as it was Katie's for asking. She was always there for her, and this minor thing was no big deal, until now. She used her forefinger to push around the skin on her face, testing to see what she would look like if she had a face lift or something. That is until Katie herself came around the corner and gave her a short laugh.

"What the hell are you doing to your face, Sierra?" She said it with what remained of her scratchy voice.

"I'm looking at it, I wish I was more... I don't know, exotic or something." She continued to poke and prod.

"Why would you want to be exotic? You're beautiful the way you are." Katie made her way across the room. "I really appreciate this Sierra, it's a one-time thing, I told my mother I would go... and you know how she is." She rolled her eyes as she said it. Asking you to pretend you're me on a blind date is too much to ask, I know."

"I don't mind at all. I never get to go out, especially to a nice place like Giovanni's. Are you worried you will get found out somehow?" Sierra stopped long enough to glance at Katie, who was rifling through the make-up pile.

"No, Mom doesn't even know what he looks like or anything. She set this up for a friend of a friend or something. The guy's mother is desperate for him to find a nice girl and settle down because he's somewhat of a playboy. The only reason I agreed to this blind date was because I owe her for missing my cousin, Owen's wedding. I just wish I could have found a way out of it without dragging you through it."

Sierra glanced at Katie. "It's okay. This interview you have could really be a big break for you. You can't risk missing it by going on a blind date with a guy your mother fixed you up with. I understand, and like I said... free food. Who goes out on a Thursday night, though?" She gave her a smile.

Katie giggled. "So what are you wearing? Oh, and I'll do your make-up, maybe make you look more exotic!" They laughed together as they set out to getting Sierra ready for her date. They also had to figure out how to make the guy think that Sierra is really Katie.

An hour later, Sierra turned to take a long look at herself in the mirror. She was transfixed on her appearance. The Sierra she looked at everyday was gone, and in her place was a beautiful woman. Her hair, normally full of curls when left, down, had been straightened and now felt like silk on her shoulders. Her freckles were hidden and her eyes were the focal point of her face. Katie used her skills to give Sierra's eyes a dark and dusky look and she added some pink to her cheeks. Her dark lips only needed a hint of color, and she was definitely a different woman.

"Are you gonna stand there and look at yourself all night or go get this silly date over with?" Katie was equally made up for her interview. The two of them stood side by side, staring at the mirror.

"I don't even look like... well me." Sierra giggled.

"Well, tonight you're not you, you're me." Katie said simply as she picked up her bag to go. "Don't forget, meet him at the entrance at 7pm. He said he would have a red handkerchief in his jacket." Katie walked over to reassure Sierra once more. "I really do appreciate it girl." She gave her one last smile and she headed out. After Katie left, Sierra slipped on the tall black pumps Katie pushed on her to go with her outfit. She took a deep breath, and with a sigh, she left for the restaurant.

A.J. was frustrated. His latest business merger was in trouble, he was in desperate need of a woman and lastly, he had this blasted date tonight that he didn't want to go on. The day was dragging and he wanted to go. He flicked open the black book on the top of his desk and sighed. He had an unusual appetite and he needed something new, something exciting to help him calm down. This company... his company was everything to him. He built it from the ground up, and with it, he become an important figurehead in the community. The truth was they didn't really know him.

He had a dark side, one he kept hidden and he needed more. His appointments were short today. One merger meeting. Tomorrow morning he had one charity appearance for a donation he had made locally. He was always glad when the corporation could donate funds in the city where it was needed. It was almost a penance for the side of him that he couldn't control. He owed his mother his life and so, from time to time when she would request this of him, he would do it, to soothe her worried soul about the playboy reputation he had developed. He checked his reflection in the mirror and smiled to himself.

He was a playboy, and that suited him just fine. There were far too many women out there for him to have to settle for just one. He loved them all, and enjoyed his life exactly as it was. The unfortunate thing was that he was an only child and his mother was constantly on him about settling down and finding a nice girl to marry, to carry on the family name.

He gave his hair one last smoothing down before he put on his glasses and made his way to the waiting car. One of the perks of running a multi-million dollar company was the luxury of enjoying someone else driving you to and from.

He would be lying if he said he didn't get a thrill of impressing the ladies by having a driver when he pulled up to a new club in town. He liked to be impressive and his looks helped with that. He took care of himself, working out 5 days a week until he was toned. He had jet black hair, almost shaved on the sides and longer on top. His eyes were described as black by most and he always had a shadowed goatee. He was the epitome of tall, dark and handsome, and his evasive nature with women gave him an air of mystery.

He settled into the cool leather of the seats and leaned back to rest for a second. Hopefully, this night would go smoothly. The last time he went out with one of his mother's "girls" she bored him to tears until they made it back to his penthouse. There, she became a tigress and the sex was phenomenal. It was typical of his situation. More often than not, these girls would come in, hoping to find a husband and he would charm them right out of their clothes before they knew what happened.

This date would be the same, of that he was sure. He felt the car come to a stop and he made his way to the restaurant with ease. He gave the hot little hostess a smile and she started shuffling the papers in front of her as she blushed. It was almost too easy for him. What he wanted most was a challenge, something to work for, at least a little. He was led to a table in the corner, as requested , and he waited. As usual, he arrived early so that he could watch and decipher the woman his mother sent for him this time. It was almost like an animal stalking its prey. He leaned back some and waited with hooded lids.

Sierra took a deep breath before entering the restaurant. She was nervous that her date would find out that she really wasn't Katie. She knew she wasn't a mess since she was receiving appreciative looks from random men in the main entrance. She was led to a table, thanked the young lady who seated her, and turned to meet this month's "guy." She felt the blood in her veins warm up and her mouth go dry at the same time. He stood and extended a hand to her, helping her into her seat. She felt the faint presence of his fingers trace her back as he helped push her seat in. Before she choked on the water she was sipping, she decided to speak first.

"So, you must be A.J?" She took another sip.

Surprised by her forwardness, he raised an eyebrow. "I assume that makes you Katie. Yes, I am A.J. It's nice to meet you."

He had a voice that spilled out of his mouth like honey. She knew exactly why he was getting appreciative glances from the waitresses. He was almost too attractive. He had classic good looks with a mix of ruggedness which made it clear that he was no innocent poster boy, but rather a force to be reckoned with.

"It's very nice to meet you too. This is a nice restaurant. Do you come here often?" She was trying making small talk, and he knew she was nervous. He could tell by the way she sipped her water uncontrollably.

"No, I've only been here a handful of times, but it's very good, trust me." He gave her a dashing smile and Sierra knew in his simple off-handed comment that he was going to irritate her.

It wasn't his looks. The truth of the matter was that he was the most intensely gorgeous man she ever saw. That alone gave him some kind of arrogance that reached out of him. He was put together like a package. Every piece of him from head to toe was perfect. Part of her wanted to ruffle his hair and put him in sweats. He almost seemed too well put together. He was gorgeous, but his cookie cutter life made him unattractive to her, not to mention that he was far too sure of himself. She again sipped at her water as he watched her. It was almost unnerving.

"Do I have something on my face? You seem to either be lost in thought or overly concerned with what I'm doing." She said it simply and with a smile, and enjoyed the puzzled look that crossed his face.

"No, on the contrary. I was just looking at you, Katie." He delivered his words smoothly, and she had to stop her heart from racing. He gave her a smile and she felt her stomach lurch. She was as bad as the hostess. She rolled her eyes and glanced at the menu. With any luck, this would be over soon anyway.

He leaned back into the booth, watching her intently. She was so beautiful, it was almost painful. He enjoyed the banter they were having because she wasn't like most women. She had no idea how beautiful she was and that intrigued him even more. Usually the women he went out with were all superficial and very much aware of their beauty. They ordered their food and managed to make some small talk about nothing. He knew she was nervous and that gave him some sort of excitement. She moved without thought and enjoyed her food without counting calories. The entire scene was refreshing for him. She made an idle joke about the waiter, which he found amusing and they laughed about it.

"The decorating in here reminds me of a painting. I think art is beautiful." She gave him a half smile, less concerned about his good looks now that she was three glasses of wine into the date.

"Really? Maybe we should go to the art show that's traveling into town next week. I can get tickets fairly easy, actually." He gave her a smile and she felt the warm heat travel up from the pit of her stomach. He certainly had a way with words, and with women. She saw more than one lady go by to use the restroom and his eager attempts to greet each and every one of them. Playboy all the way.

He wasn't sure why he even asked her to the art show. She was definitely not his type, and not an easy conquest either. Perhaps it was the challenge that made him want her more. He gave her every look and effort that he possibly could, and she brushed him off at every turn. Maybe he wasn't her type, but whatever it was made him want her even more. Even now, as she hummed along to the ambient music in the restaurant, he wanted to kiss her full pouting mouth. He felt his pants tighten and he knew she would be his before they were through. Soon, dinner was over and they made their way outside. He walked her to her car and waited for her to look up at him.

"Well, I guess I'm gonna go." She gave a hiccup and a giggle, and he knew she wasn't going anywhere. He walked her over to the area where his driver was and after a moment of tapping on the roof, he safely tucked her into his car.

"Sorry, sweetheart, but you're not driving anywhere." He let his hand linger for a moment on her waist.

She was full of fire. "You can't kidnap me A.J. No way, Jose." She fell into a fit of giggles, then and he couldn't help but smile at her.

He felt the tension rise even more than before. As he clicked her in the seat belt, he was able to follow the line of her clinging dress up her hips and ending with a set of full breasts straining against the soft fabric, begging to be released. She looked up at him and he smiled at her. He wanted her. He knew it the second she looked up at him. There was something different and refreshing about her. Her hand trembled just slightly and he felt the heat rush through him. He let her go, watching as she straightened her clothes and looked at him.

Her heart was beating faster than usual and she wasn't sure why. He held her hand for just a second longer than necessary when he helped her in the car. He made his way around and slid into the seat beside her.

He looked up at her and leaned over closer. "I'm taking you home, you obviously cannot drive."

She felt a tremor go through her body as she felt his hot breath on her ear. He owned a really flashy car with a driver, it was one good sign, but even still, she was leery of getting into a car with someone she just met. The reality was, she didn't have much choice in the matter. She couldn't walk, let alone drive.

She gave him directions and soon enough they were at her apartment. He guided her up the stairs and soon she was inside. She felt her body come to life as he walked her inside. She watched him slide his eyes over the bed and then back to her.

"I hope you will be more careful Katie, perhaps not drink as much?" He reached out and took her hand in his.

His touch was sending little balls of fire through her veins and she knew this was dangerous ground. She felt his fingers moving along her wrist and he leaned towards her closer and closer still until she heard the front door open. Reality came crashing back in and she turned red as she glanced up at him. He stood slowly and moved towards her.

"Hey Sierra, I can't even begin to tell you how much stuff costs at the store now, I mean it's ridiculous." She stopped short at Sierra's door noticing the man inside. Sierra struggled to sit up some.

The blonde was much closer to his typical tastes. She had come bounding in full of sassiness.

Sierra gave her a look and Katie smiled. "So who is this?" She extended her perfectly manicured hand towards A.J. and he eagerly held it to his lips.

Sierra felt her face flaming as she explained the story, and how they came to end up here, now.

"Wait a second who is Sierra?" He gave them both a confused look.

"Me, I am... it's actually my middle name." Sierra gave Katie a sour look but he seemed to buy it.

"My name is Alayna, it is nice to meet you." She stifled a smile at Sierra. Alayna was actually Sierra's middle name. This was getting more complicated by the moment.

There was a moment of silence that passed between them before he took a step towards Sierra. He watched her for a moment as she struggled to stand, somehow trying to put herself together. She gave Katie an apologetic look.

"Well, I have to go back out, Katie, I'm glad your home safe, and A.J. thank you taking such good care of her. You two have a good evening." She winked at an angry Sierra before leaving the apartment.

He gave Alayna a wave and once she was gone, he turned to look at her. She wasn't sure what to do or feel. The alcohol in her system was more than she should have taken in and it had impaired her judgement. It didn't matter what she wanted really as he made his way over to her and leaned in close before his mouth made its descent on hers. He pulled her towards him and explored her mouth at length. He was radiating heat and she met his kiss with equal intensity. They moved together with him pushing her back into the couch and holding her arms above her head with one arm. He ran his hands under the hem of her dress and up along her thigh, she wanted him to touch her, but yet she didn't. He found the laced edge of her panties and she froze, finally coming to her senses. She was anticipating his touch when her phone rang, shattering the moment. What the hell, she inwardly cursed herself?

He stood now, facing her and looking down at her. He wasn't upset, but merely amused. He wanted her, eventually, but never like this. He stood once more and made his way to the door. Leaving her with an aching need she felt deep down and nothing to cure it. She glanced down at her clothes and straightened them quickly. What was wrong with her anyway? She always had control over her actions, but today she most definitely was not in control. What he must think of her, meeting him on a blind date and then within an hour letting him touch her like that.

"I'll pick you up next Friday at 8pm Katie, be ready, I can be impatient." He rebuttoned his jacket and smoothed his hair before dropping a quick peck on her forehead and leaving her stunned.

"What was he even talking about anyway?" she whispered to herself once he had left.

She hung her head in her hands and sighed. She had very strict rules about sex, and dating and right now she was breaking every one of them. She allowed herself a moment to try and recover, but she had been changed for good. Whatever she did, she would need to stay away from A.J.

The next week passed by and she did her best to stay calm and not think about him. Katie was making it nearly impossible with her line of questioning that seemed endless.

"Oh wow so you kissed him, that's it? Honey, he is gorgeous, I should have totally went on that date." She laughed at her own joke but seemingly aware of Sierra's unhappiness.

"Yes, and it was stupid because he is an ass, totally shallow and he thinks he is some gift put here for women to look at." She rolled her eyes. "Not to mention, he kissed that night's version of me, not the real me." She threw her bag into the window of the car.

"Maybe he is a playboy, and shallow and whatever, but the truth of the matter is he liked you Sierra, and when was the last time you went out and had any fun anyway? It's good for you, go enjoy it." She made her way to her car. "Byeee." She gave a wave.

"Whatever, be quiet Katie." She said it with a laugh as she settled into her car. It was then she noticed the note that was under the wiper. She moved to retrieve it.

That was only the beginning, I want you
She felt her body come to life with the excitement of the words. He certainly had no problem sharing what he wanted, but she had decided to not let it go any further than it already had. She had very strict guidelines about how she lived her life. She had been reckless and let the fantasy take over yesterday. It had been the make-up, the dress and the stupid wine. Nothing more. She wouldn't let it happen a second time. She needed to focus on the important things in life like her family, and taking care of herself. She made her way towards the town where she had grown up. She was off this morning and was going to see her little brother off to his first day of school. She loved the small town charm that made up the community where she used to live. It was hard to imagine that just two towns over the city was overfilled with people and congestion. It was good to sometimes come home and put things into perspective. She only hoped to not run into A.J., ever. He had wanted that woman from dinner, not the one getting ready to visit her family in a sundress and flip flops. The fantasy was something she couldn't give him, or anyone for that matter. All she had to do was get refocused.

She saw her little brother in the front yard with their father and she got out of the car just in time to hop into the SUV that would take the four of them to the school. He was excited, and scared, she could tell by the way he was fidgety but not talking much. Having a child after so many years since Sierra had been a struggle for her parents, but they loved Jacob more than anything in the world. He had been a miracle child for them really, and completely unexpected. She had been 16 when he was born and the shock had just subsided about having a new toddler running around when he was getting ready to go to school. Even harder was the fact that her brother needed medication for his condition. When he was five he had been diagnosed with myeloid leukemia. The medication alone had cost her father their savings. She knew she needed to do something to help, but she wasn't sure what. She looked down at her brother and put her hand on his knee and he moved his to hers smiling, then after a second she tapped his nose and he would tap hers back. Finally, she stuck out her tongue and he followed suit. He relaxed as she tickled him in the back seat.

The brick building was spread out ranch style and had two wings. It was a beautiful undertaking and after years it was finally ready. She walked hand in hand with Jacob, her father ahead of them. He really was a good boy. They watched as the announcer made a speech about the importance of family. It was then that she froze. She heard his voice before she even looked down towards the podium. He was dressed impeccably as he had been yesterday. He was far away enough that he did see her but she watched him as he shared the importance of meeting educational goals. That was where she had recognized his name. Trager Enterprises was the largest business in the area and often would give money to local causes. It was his money that made this building possible. The old school had been falling apart and now, apparently with his help, they had a new one, one that had a special wing for children with illness like Jacob. She felt her heart soften a little towards him. This knowledge would only make it that much harder to stay away from him.

She walked with Jacob and her father to his class. She felt the sense of loss once he was inside for them both. She only wished her mother could have been there to see him go inside. Just two years ago, she was killed in a tragic car accident that left her and her father with Jacob. They did the best they could and now he was getting older. Her father headed back to the car and she waited a few seconds longer wanting to remember this moment for her mother. She turned to leave and there he was, leaning against the wall watching her again.

"Hello Katie." He enunciated her name strangely and gave her a stormy look.

"Mr. Trager hello... again. My brother is a student here now. This is a great thing you did." She knew she was rambling and gave him one final look. "It was nice to see you again." As she walked by him, he grabbed her arm pulling her towards him.

He kissed her lightly and let her go, it was almost a tease, but enough to remind her that he was in control. She started walking as soon as she was free and she tried to calm her racing heart as she did it. She saw his dark smile as he turned to leave. He was the most arrogant person she had ever met that she knew. She touched her fingertips to her lips still tingling from his latest onslaught. How was it he managed to show up places when she was there?

She headed to lunch with her father before heading back into town. They had just sat down when suddenly he was there. She almost choked on her water.

"Sierra, Mr. Trager is having lunch with us. It seems we he knows you and in mentioning lunch I asked him to join us." She smiled weakly and looked up to catch his eye. It was as if he were looking right through her.

"How nice." It was all she could manage to squeak out.

"Sierra, are you okay, you looked pale." Her father seemed genuinely concerned.

"Yes, you look as though something shocked you or something of that nature." He interjected with the same smile that drove her crazy.

"I'm fine, just some pesky bugs in the hall before that's all." She saw his smile again but he said nothing.

Lunch was an interesting time. He spoke and laughed with her father as if there was nothing underlying between them. He asked her to show him the gardens at the café and at her father's insistence she did.

"You look beautiful today Miss Ford." He glanced over at her as they walked.

"Thank you Mr. Trager." She refused to look at him.

"So, when were you going to tell me that you are not Katie?" He never broke stride.

"How did you find out?" She crossed her arms over the front of her dress as they walked.

"Does that really matter? The reality is you lied, I don't do well with liars." He said it stiffly. She felt the anger start to rise deep down.

"Oh really, well, it's a good thing it was only one date." She flashed her eyes at him and saw him do his best to hide a smile.

"Have I mentioned how badly I want you?" she tripped lightly and he caught her arm.

"Really? Why would you say something like that to me?" She stopped to look at him.

"It's simply the truth, if I want something I find it much easier to get if I simply make it clear." He took a step towards her and she started walking again as he chuckled.

"You're safe for now, Miss Ford. One day soon I won't keep that promise." She glanced at him, but he continued to look at the pond beside them.

"Your almost a different person today Sierra, more free and happy perhaps."

"I am in my own clothes, and I'm at home. I supposed I am free that way." He stopped her and looked down into her face.

"I like you better this way." There was a long moment between them and she broke free and made her way up the path. He chuckled.

"Tell me about your brother."

There was something in the way he said it that made her feel close to him. He seemed genuinely interested and she shared her story with him. Her brother had been diagnosed with a form of leukemia. He listened and interjected when necessary. He was almost a different person in this environment. She found him easy to talk to and strangely, she felt safe with him. He spoke about some of the new directions the company was going in and she listened, interested in the way business is managed. She gave him some input and he arched an eyebrow at her point of view.

She was happy she had at least shown more to her character than the way she behaved around him before. Right before they made their way back to the café he stopped and pushed her into the overhang kissing her again, quickly but deep and hard. He stopped and pulled away slightly before he backed away completely. They made their way back to the table where her father sat and Trager jumped right back into the conversation as if it were nothing. They parted ways and she rode back with her father to get her car.

"That Mr. Trager is a nice guy, Sierra." She looked over and he gave her a wink.

"He is an ass dad, plain and simple." She crossed her arms in the car and he smiled at her but didn't say another word.

She missed home when she wasn't there, but she loved the city more. She said her goodbyes to her father and headed back to the apartment. She pulled her car into the lot adjacent to her apartment building and her phone started ringing. She assumed it was A.J. and ignored it since her hands were full. The second time it went off after she had been inside for a few minutes she checked it. It was work, with a sigh, she called Harry back at the diner.

"Sure Harry, I'll be there just as soon as I can ok?" With a sigh she pulled her hair back into a bun and threw on her uniform. Hopefully since it was a Friday she would make decent tips.

The night seemed to drag on as she made her usual rounds. Despite her effort to not think about him, he was there and present in her mind. Maybe Katie was right, maybe she needed to get out more, and have fun. Things had been a mess since Jake and she couldn't seem to move past it. There was some level of trust she couldn't seem to give too freely to anyone. She was tired and she was unhappy. Sure, she had great friends, but she was living paycheck to paycheck and she needed to get things together. Her classes here and there were certainly not helping to propel her career in any way. She had big plans once upon a time and now she was just surviving. She felt someone touch her apron and glanced back to see another staggering drunk trying to touch her rear. She pulled the apron away and made her way to the counter. She let her head hang in her hands for a second refusing to give in to the stress, she was only 26 she still had time to get it together. Finally, the night came to a close and she headed home lost in deep thought about her future.

The next morning was there too quickly and she rolled over with a sigh. Today would be busy. The only day the she could actually clean the apartment and get it together. They both worked and went to school all week and rarely got anything done. She knew that Katie was still sleeping. She shuffled her way to the kitchen lost in thought once more about her brother. His prognosis, if medicated was good, but she worried about him. She looked around and jumped in full force. She would be lying if she said she didn't think about him. It was strange, someone making her feel things now. She had assumed that was all behind her. She wanted desperately to be like Katie. To find love and happiness, but none of it was for her. She needed to focus on what was important.

A.J. was having a similar morning. He was killing himself waiting to find a woman. Usually he could go out and find any number of them to bring home, but now he was stuck. He told himself it had nothing to do with her, but he wasn't so sure. Ever since their kiss at the school opening he couldn't get her out of his head. This was the first day in a long time he woke up unsatisfied from the night before. He always had someone, but she had robbed him of it. He was completely focused on winning her over. He wanted her even now, in his bed. He gritted his teeth and made his way to the shower. Sometimes it helped, sometimes not. Soon, however, she would be his even if only for one night.

The rest of the morning flew by and Sierra looked around enjoying her clean apartment. There was a sense of pride in that and she liked order. She never would be considered spontaneous on any level. She slumped down in the chair and threw the rag in she had in the waiting basket. Soon Katie would be gone, moving for her new job, and she would either have to find a way to make the payments on this place herself, or move home. She liked the simplicity of the apartment, but she was doubtful there was any way she could make it on her own. For now she would enjoy it.

He knew she would be mad. Furious more likely. She wanted him as much as he wanted her, but she was determined to fight him. She was always leery of him, part of him liked it that way, and he enjoyed the banter they seemed to find themselves in every time they spoke. She was smart and quick, he knew that by talking to her, but something kept her from giving in to him and he wanted to know what it was. He wanted her and he rarely was ever turned down. She was fighting him and the chase had begun. When she was here, which he was sure would be within the hour, he had every intention of claiming her body once and for all. The morning seemed to go on forever as he anticipated the way she would feel beneath him. He wanted to control her every move and the thought flooded him with fire. Soon, he thought to himself, soon.

He heard the first stirrings of activity in the lobby. He smiled and leaned back in his chair waiting and anticipating how she would look when she was angry. He spun around as his assistant opened his door.

Mr. Trager someone, a young lady is here to see you. "She glanced behind her quickly. "She said you were expecting her."

"I am, please let her in." He sat up and made every effort to look busy as she stormed into the room.

As soon as he heard the click of the door, he looked up at her and it hit him like a punch to the gut. She was more beautiful at this very moment than she had been yet. Her hair was a swirling mass of reds and browns and flowed down her back freely. He could almost feel his fingers itch to run through it. Her arms were crossed and her body was fitted into a dress that hugged her every curve and angle.

"What the hell were you thinking towing my car?" She continued to tap her foot as she waved a sheet of paper at him. "I had to take a cab to get here and even that took forever. I can't afford to take a cab all the way across town, Trager." She huffed and exhaled slowly and he noticed the pink hue of her cheeks,

"I'm sorry Sierra, I wanted you to come see me, and I knew this was one way to make it happen." He leaned back and smiled.

"You are so smug sometimes, A.J., you just assume the world is here to give you whatever you want aren't you?" She was practically yelling and he wanted to somehow bottle up all the fire she carried and make love to her for hours.

"Sometimes, yes. I like getting what I want and right now I want you." He said it simply enough, but there was much more to the statement.

"You don't even know me, Trager." She sighed.

It was the truth and it had never been clearer to her than right now. He had no idea of what was on her plate, or in her world for that matter.

She was already stretched too thin and it wouldn't take much to push her over the edge. Her Monday started out badly, her car was towed, and she'd spent hours on the phone looking for various agencies to help fund Jacobs's medication. Money was running out and she needed a solution fast. Her father called her to discuss the house and he decided to take out a loan against it. It was the only thing of value he had left that he'd shared with her mother. With the growing figures for Jacobs's medication, it was clear he had no choice. Then after going outside and seeing that her car was missing, she stomped off in search for it, only to find it had been a ruse to get her here.

> "I want you in my arms Sierra. I have wanted to touch you since that night when I watched you walk into the restaurant."

> "I don't know how you do it, Trager, but for me, I am not interested in becoming some notch on your headboard."

> "I don't have a headboard, Sierra, but you will see soon enough." His arrogance was stifling, but she couldn't stop the warmth that spread through her body. "I know you want the very same thing from me but you won't let yourself go. I am not asking for marriage or family, I just want you, plain and simple."

He was almost too much to look at. He was impeccably dressed as always. He delivered his point clearly and effectively and she knew what he said was true. She wasn't too old yet to want to be touched by someone, and held by someone. The obvious problem was that she wasn't that type of girl.

> "Shut the door, Sierra." She did as he told her, and as she started to walk towards him, he added "lock it."

With a gulp she did as she was told. There was an underlying current in the air and she could tell he was playing with her, like a cat and mouse game. She wouldn't be bossed around by his arrogance and she wanted him to know it. The entire situation was out of hand and she let it go too far that day in her apartment. She took responsibility for drinking the wine that got her into this mess.

"Mr. Trager, I think I need to apologize. I think I may have given you the wrong impression about me. I am not the kind of girl who just lets strange men touch her... well you know what I mean. I can't let this... attraction between us continue." She fumbled the words out. "To say that my life is complicated right now would be a very sincere understatement."

They sounded less harsh than she intended, but she finally got them out. He turned slowly towards her and he had a sinister look about him. He wasn't frowning, or smiling, but it was as if he was stuck between both. He moved towards her like a cat chasing its prey and she backed up against his desk as he moved over her. He was slow at first. He simply ran his finger across her neck relishing at her quick intake of breath. He looked at her as he traced his finger across her chest and across the tops of her breasts. She couldn't breathe, it was if she had never said a word. He kissed the tops of each mound lightly before he undid her hair, letting it cascade around her like a fiery blanket. He put his hands in it and pulled her hard against him, crushing his mouth to hers. She was lost. The feel of his mouth, grinding into hers was a welcome one. She tried to put up a defense against him and failed. He turned her around and she felt him lean into her as he whispered into her ear.

"Sierra, I have been very clear about the fact that I want you. I want you to know that before anything else happens. I want you to know without any doubt that it's going to happen." She gasped as he pushed against her and she could feel the length of him against her.

"You have to let go, let yourself feel all of the things I want to show you." He kissed her mouth lightly. "If you want to say no I will, but understand if you do, I may not try again."

She nodded yes to him as the rest of her defense slipped away. He was very matter-of-fact about things and she loved it. She felt him unzip her dress and trail his fingers down her spine as the dress slipped to the floor. She was aware of every nerve ending in her body as his hands reached around and touched her.

"Don't move." It was all he told her before he began his descent.

Even in slow motion Sierra couldn't stop the kiss, she welcomed it more than she should have and she shivered as she felt his other hand under the other side of her head. He raised back only once searching her face and seeing no resistance, he kissed her once more. This time deeper, longer and more demanding. She felt him cup the back of her head to tilt her towards him as the kiss intensified.

She didn't want to fight anymore, couldn't fight anymore. She stood and with one zip she let her dress drop to the floor leaving him speechless. She made her way over to him and he felt her tentatively put her mouth on his. This kind of forwardness was completely out of her comfort zone and he knew it.

"How long has it been Sierra?" Her eyes flew open to look at him.

"Four years." She whispered it to him and it almost pushed him over the edge.

She let him love her in a way she had never known. Most of it was undoubtedly because of his experience as a lover. There was a sense of panic she'd felt when he told her there may not be another chance. She wanted to feel good, feel better. Her life was a mix of stress and planning and all she wanted was to feel something else. His skin on hers was like fire and ice and she let go, of her fears, of her stress of everything and he loved her completely. She met his every move and every action and she knew she was giving him as much as he gave her.

A.J. was moved by what had happened between them. He had certainly been with many women, but nothing had ever been as moving as what they had shared. She had always been distant and scared and yet something switched and she gave instead herself to him with everything in her power. She wasn't shy or meek, she was eager and demanding and he enjoyed pushing her to her limits. Yet, as good as it was, she was holding back something he couldn't quite put his finger on. She lay cupped in front of him and he could sense she was exhausted and simply didn't want to move. It wasn't usually his style, cuddling, but for her he would make an exception. There was a sense of sadness about her he wanted to fix, despite the warning bells in his head. He traced his finger up and down the length of her arm as she dozed slightly. No, this wasn't his usual situation on any level at all. It happened almost simultaneously, the two of them remembering where they were. Sierra jumped up to start gathering her clothes. To be honest, the fact that they were in his office was mortifying and she was blushing the entire time. Along the way that fact had slipped her mind, until now.

"Sierra... Sierra calm down it's fine." He smiled at her as she continued to slip back into her clothes and he was able to be a bystander and admire the curve of her hip and the softness of her skin as the light hit it.

"No A.J. it's not alright. This is not me, I mean not really me." She was frantic in her actions and after he redressed, he stilled her arms and helped her to breath. He sensed a panic in her, something deep down.

"Do you want to talk about it Sierra?" he brushed her hair back from her face as he cupped her chin lovingly.

"No, no I'm fine, I'm sorry. I have to go." She gave him one last look and headed out of the office in a hurry. Something was wrong and he wanted to know what it was.

She took the few strides to reach her building and once inside her room, she collapsed against the door. What was she thinking? No matter what she did, she somehow managed to make the situation worse. She shook her head to clear her thoughts of him and what had happened, and called home. Her father answered and they took some time to discuss the home loan further. He sounded tired and she worried about him. She also spoke with Jacob about school. He was excited about the teacher and his class. She missed his little face all the time. She listened to her father and told him about work and Katie, she failed to mention Trager. They chatted for a while discussing the options she had once Katie was gone. Her last day at work was yesterday and she would be another week packing and getting things ready before leaving. Finally, they hung up and she carefully stood to walk into the kitchen. She blushed, remembering. Even now, she was sore from what he put her through. She had to remind herself that it could never happen again. She took a drink of water and settled into the armchair in the living room. Katie had been gone for hours, having met a friend in town. For the next few hours she had the place to herself and she planned to use them wisely. She started running a bath, touching the hot water with her fingertips. She was soaking for ten minutes before she heard a loud thump on the front door. She sat up quickly and wrapped herself in a robe. She felt her heart beating fast as she made her way to the front door. She checked the eye hole and saw no one. She froze when she saw the shadow of someone in the hall.

She opened the door to look. He stood back looking at her.

"Sierra, hey look don't shut the door." He rushed towards her block it with his arm.

She folded her arms. "What do you want Brandon, why are you here and

Furthermore, how did you know I was here?" He pushed the door slightly and came inside.

She took a step back, this was part of the problem between them. He scared her. With A.J., she knew he wouldn't hurt her. With Brandon, it made her worry, about her safety.

He reached out to her. "Sierra, I miss you so much, if you would just let me show you." He took a step towards her and she moved out of his reach, grabbing the vase on the table and moving away.

"Brandon, please. You know it's done with us you can't do this. I need you to go." She moved towards the door and he grabbed her arm. She knew there would be bruises tomorrow. It was then that the front door opened and Katie came through it, followed by someone she had never met.

It was obvious they had walked into something dicey and the man with Katie spoke up first. "Is there a problem here?"

Katie made her way over to Sierra hugging her as she walked her towards the kitchen.

"No man, not a thing, I was just going. Sierra, I'll be back." Brandon said as he left and he shut the door.

Sierra was visibly shaken, she had never expected him to follow her here. She had thought to leave him behind and start over.
"Thanks, I appreciate the help." She glanced over at Katie.

"Sierra this is Marcus, a good friend of mine." She gave Marcus a huge smile and Sierra shook his hand.

"No wonder you sent me on that crazy date." She gave them both a half smile, still reeling from Brandon's visit. "Really though, thanks for your help. She excused herself to go think.

She made her way to her room. She had no choice, she would have to go home now, and at least with her father around, she felt safe. She supposed she could call the police, but she wasn't sure much would come of it. Instead, she focused on her assignment for the class she was taking online. Monday, she would give a notice at the diner.

Brandon didn't bother her anymore the rest of the week. Two of her tires were slashed on Friday morning and she was beginning to wonder if it was Brandon all along. She had Katie drop her off at the diner. She would normally be happy and carefree, but now she was depressed and wasn't sure how to get out of the way she felt. More than that, she was scared and worried about where she was headed. The day went by quickly and she made her way home on the bus, hoping to just get there safely. She jumped when her phone rang and she checked the number and relaxed. It wasn't Brandon.

"Hello A.J., how are you?"

"I'm doing well, I was hoping maybe we could talk, before our date tonight."

She frowned, thinking, she had not only forgotten about the date, some part of her assumed he had been joking anyway. Given the last time they had seen each other she almost figured she wouldn't hear from him again.

"About that A.J., I'm not sure if I can. Some things have come up I need to take care of. Besides, I don't have a car."

"Even better, I'll send you one, are you at home?"

"Yes, but…"

"Give me thirty minutes." He cut her off mid-sentence and then hung up abruptly.

The truth of the matter was that she wasn't sure if she could handle seeing him right now. With the possibility of Brandon lurking about, she was consumed with worry. A.J. probably never had these kinds of issues. On top of her own problems, she was concerned about her father and Jacob. Based on her calculations, even with taking out a loan on the house, he would need more money down the road. What would they do then? She considered A.J., not for the first time either. If she could somehow get him to fall for her then she would have the financial freedom to help Jacob, but it was completely out of character for her to do something like that. Even still, the idea burned in the back of her mind. She couldn't admit to herself even now, that she may want to get him to fall for her because she just wanted to be with him, it was ridiculous to even think it. He was a known playboy and he would never settle for her no matter what she wanted, on the surface or deep down.

True to his word a car arrived to pick her up. She made the attempt to put on something nice. She had on a black dress and heels and her hair was spun up on top of her head. She applied her make–up, much as Katie had done before, but just not as much. She sat back to see how she looked and once again the person staring back was a stranger. She would at least try to test the waters, to see if he felt anything for her. They had only known each other a short time, but there was something there and they both knew it. She watched the buildings fly by, lost in her own thoughts. Nothing made sense anymore. A.J. Trager had her head spinning and it wouldn't allow for her to focus on what was important. She would test the waters, so to speak, to see what he said and felt about her. She had zero powers of seduction up her sleeve, but she would try, for Jacob. The car pulled up to his building and she made her way inside and up to his floor. Since he towed her car, she knew exactly where to find him now, he had been nice enough to send her money back to her for the car and the tow with a courier, but it was still about the principle. She smiled at his assistant, a blonde who was gorgeous, and couldn't help but wonder if he slept with her too.

She heard his voice welcome her in and she took a deep breath and went inside. He looked up from the papers on his desk and sat back in his chair. He was all business-like and the air that surrounded him seemed to come to life. She glanced at the desk and gulped. Just a few days ago, she was laid out in that very spot. She felt the redness rush to her cheeks.

A.J. looked her over. He usually had a firm handle on his behavior, but he struggled with not finding her since she had last been here. Not even 30 minutes after she left during her last visit, he felt himself wanting her again. She was under his skin and he was trying to figure out how to handle it. Something was very different today, she was as pale as a ghost and almost lifeless despite her efforts to seem calm and carefree. He tried to push down the need to fix whatever was bothering her. Instead he stood and walked towards her.

She saw him coming and despite her fears she felt the fire almost immediately. He made her come to life and feel safe all at the same time. He stopped and leaned back on the desk.

"Come here, Sierra." She obeyed him. He lifted his hand up to her pale face and traced the line of her jaw with his forefinger. "Did you think about me about what we did?" She nodded her head yes and her eyes met his. He frowned because she was not completely here with him, not now.

"What's wrong Sierra?"

"Nothing, why do you ask." She gave him a warm smile and reached up to run her fingers over his sports coat.

He frowned. She was doing her best to appear seductive, but her actions didn't match her appearance. There was something going on but she was hiding it from him, toying with him. There was a loud bang from the outer office and she practically jumped into his arms. She buried her head in his chest and instinctively he wrapped his arms around her.

His door opened to reveal his assistant. "Sorry about the commotion, Mr. Trager. The Adams kids were here and they decided to play a prank on Dad. They have since left and Mr. Adams apologized for their behavior." She gave him a quick glance and took in the scene of him holding that nice girl whose car he had towed.

"Thank you for letting us know." He gave her a smile and once the door was shut, he addressed the woman who was wrapped around him.

"Okay, Sierra, what's going on, what's wrong?" She pulled away from him.

"Nothing is wrong, A.J... I just had a rough night and I apologize for my behavior. I didn't mean to embarrass you like that." She sniffed and he frowned at her.

"No, I'm not letting this go Sierra, I want to know why you are trembling like that, and now!" He was demanding and loud and she worried someone would hear them outside of the doors.

"I may as well tell you, there has been a situation that has come up and I will be moving in a week or so. I guess I'm just nervous or stressed, that's all." She trembled slightly as he took her hand in his and turned it over, lightly tracing the palm with his thumb.

He pulled her to him and she welcomed the arms that wrapped around her, holding her. She knew then she could never seduce him. Hell, she wasn't even able to have a conversation with him without falling apart. She felt his hands rubbing her back and she closed her eyes, enjoying the way his hands felt. He moved them now, running them down the length of her and she trembled now, not from fear, but of what she knew his hands would do to her if she didn't stop them now. She tried to pull away from him, but he held her there and she looked up at him.

"Didn't you like what I did the other day to you, Sierra?" He pulled her arm up and nibbled his way up the underside of her forearm. "Answer me, Sierra."

"Yes." She whispered the words as her body reacted to him. She had all the strength in the world when he wasn't in front of her. When he was she was lost to him.

"Is your family in trouble?" He continued up her arm having moved around to the top of her shoulder now.

"No, well yes, but no." She frowned, unsure how to answer him.

"Then you can't leave me, I'm not done with you yet." He pulled her face to his and kissed her roughly, needing to feel the softness of her full red lips beneath his.

She knew she had no choice, she had to go, but right now she was here, with him... safe. He pulled back and without thought she pulled his head back down to hers. Without warning, he stopped and backed away from her. She trembled, watching his face and took a step back.

"I have to touch you Sierra, do you understand? I have thought of nothing else." He moved back towards her and pulled her towards him by the arm. She whimpered and he let her go. He may be passionate, but he would never hurt her. He gently pulled the arm out of the sleeve she was wearing, despite her protests and looked at the black and purple bruise forming on her arm. He felt the rage well up inside him and knew he wanted someone to hurt for this.

"Who did this to you, Sierra?" She looked at the floor and shoved her arm back in her sleeve to go. He grabbed her chin, forcing her to look at him. "Who?"

She knew he wouldn't give in until she answered him. "He is an ex, I moved because of him and he found me." She watched the play of emotions on his face as he stood. "Don't move Sierra, I mean it." He walked over to the window and she stood rooted to the spot. He was on the phone talking to someone and when he was through he made his way back over to her.

"My driver is on his way here, you are to let him take you to my place where I know you will be safe and wait for me until later."

"Mr. Trager, that's not necessary, this is not your problem, it's mine." She stood to go, but felt him move between her and the door.

"Sierra, I am not arguing with you about this? Where is your car I'll have it brought to your house."

"You sent a car for me, remember? Someone slashed my tires." She said it dryly and he swore under his breath. There was a knock on the door and he simply said "Open."

He spoke to his driver for a moment before he walked over to her. He was almost gentle in the way he led her to the door. "I will see you there later." He stopped and turned her around to face him. "Tell me you will be there Sierra, I don't have time to worry about you all afternoon."

She knew he was serious and she would do as she asked. "Yes, I'll be there A.J..." As the driver left the room, he pulled her into a kiss. "I'll be there soon."

"Where am I going, A.J.?" she asked it simply but he knew she needed to feel safe.

"To my place, you will be safe there." At her hesitation he added. "Just do this... for me." She looked up at him and knew he was sincere, she nodded her head yes. He kissed the top of her head as she left.

She made her way down the elevator and to the waiting car. She planned to seduce him, to help her family. Somewhere along the way she simply planned to tell him she was leaving. As usual, he took over the conversation and made the decisions for her. She visibly relaxed in the seat. She needed to feel safe for a little while anyway. She knew she would be gone in a few hours, but for right now she would be at his house, where her ex can't find her.

Nothing prepared her for the penthouse where he lived. It was obvious to her that he had refined and elegant tastes in everything. From the marbled counters, to the floor to ceiling windows. She felt out of place here, like a dirty stray puppy or something. The driver, she found out on her way here, had been working for Trager for two years and was close to him. He led her to the main room where she could relax. Twenty minutes later he returned with a box in hand.

"What's this?" She took the box and lifted the lid slightly. Once she saw the lace, she closed it immediately.

"Mr. Trager said to make sure you were fed and had something to wear. He also ordered food for dinner and it will be here before he arrives.

"You have full use of the house, Miss Ford." He tipped his hat and left her. She spun around the room and set about exploring. She found a huge bedroom with a canopied bed, and adjacent to it was a marbled bathroom. To say it was elegant was an understatement. She filled the large oval bathtub and decided to slip in and try to enjoy it. She redressed in her work clothes. The "outfit" he gave her was a sexy lacy thing, barely there. It was a dark blue color and he tucked a note inside that read:

I will be there at 6, wear this... and your hair down.

She had to smile, he was so demanding and yet it suited him. She thought about the next steps for her and where she would go from here. It all came back to the same conclusion. She had no choice but to go home. She lifted her arms to brush out her hair with her fingers and winced in pain, once again reminded of Brandon, and his declaration that he would be back. She heard the door and felt the same fear creep in and then she remembered the food. She checked, and opened the door to a lovely young woman with an arm load of boxes. She put them all in the warming oven and looked at the clock. It was 5:45. She decided she would wear it, for him. He was sweet enough to let her come here to feel safe. It was the least she could do. She tried to deny it had anything to do with the fact that they would be alone in his house. She also had thrown the idea of seducing him out the window. For now, she just wanted to erase the past couple of days and feel something good. She changed her clothes and waited.

He came home quietly, barely a sound. Something that didn't shock her. He moved into the room and dropped his things as he took long strides to get to the bedroom. He froze when he saw her there. Slowly he undid his tie and started undressing.

"Come here Sierra, help me." She did as he asked, watching his face as she stripped him of his clothes. His skin was tight and smooth and she ran her hands over his chest lightly before he grabbed her hands in his. He pulled her behind him and made the short trip to his bedroom. As she had imagined, the room with the marbled bathroom was his. He stopped in front of the bed and let her go.

> "Get on the bed... and then lay on your back." He said it and moved to the other side of the room to finish removing his clothes.

When she was done, she felt her heart beating out of her chest. She was laying here like a sacrifice to him. She had a need to be that for him. Whatever made him this way, whatever drove him, she didn't know. She only wanted to make him feel better, and in turn make herself feel better. He moved towards her and she lay still. She expected to see a sinister smile play across his face, but the one he had was a concerned one instead. He moved easily onto the bed, above her. Instead of ravishing her as she expected, he pulled her closer to him and held her. The action was a simple one, but necessary. She closed her eyes and felt her body relax in the warm strength of his arms. She needed this, the security of it. It wouldn't be long before even this moment was a memory, and she wanted to enjoy it for as long as she could. They lay that way for a while, his hands slowly moving along her arms and hips. His movements were not sexual but more loving than anything.

He raised above her slightly to look at her. She was beautiful and she was laying in his bed, something that never happened. He always made a point of being with women someplace else, never here. She was special, he knew it from the beginning, but what he was feeling now was new for him.

"Do you want to talk about it Sierra?" He played with an auburn curl as he looked down at her. She reached up and put her hand on his cheek.

"No, I don't want to talk, A.J. I just want to feel safe, and wanted." Their eyes made contact and the mood shifted dramatically.

"Are you sure?" He took the time to make the extra effort before he touched her like that. He was fighting his instincts already, trying to be there and trying to make her feel safe. If she opened that door on her own, welcoming him in, it would take very little before he gave her everything once more.

"Yes, I'm sure... love me, A.J."

He needed no further invitation and his mouth found her full and red lips eagerly. His actions were focused and specific, even he felt the trembling need building within. Her hair was spread across the pillow like a flame, and the lingerie he had sent fit her like a glove. He held his focus on her mouth, kissing her and feeding off of her lips until they were bruised. She touched him back, running her fingers down his back and in his hair as he kissed on her. He moved his hands down her shoulders and chest casually licking and nipping through the lace of her clothing. He nipped the skin on her belly, all the while his hands were freeing her upper body from the confinement of the outfit. He used his hands to cup and love on her until he made his way back up. It was almost painful when he would move the heat of his mouth off of her skin and move to another area. She reveled in the feel of him on her and the patterns his mouth made on her flesh... Her body was on fire. Her hands pulling his head up and back to her waiting mouth. He did as she asked and gave her a passionate kiss, drinking from her mouth. She wanted this, wanted him more now than ever. Only he could make her forget their pain and the worry of what life had in store for her. Only he could take her someplace else.

He made a leisurely trail down the rest of her body, leaving no area untouched by him. Suddenly stood back to look at her naked form splayed across the bed. She felt no shame in it, in this moment she belonged to him.

"You are mine, Sierra, do you understand that... only mine." She nodded to him and he smiled at her before making a trail up her thighs with his mouth. Soon it was too much, the way he touched her, the way he loved her. She wanted to be in this moment for as long as possible

He moved above her and she felt the joining of their body's like a tidal wave. He felt the heat of her envelop him and he stopped, waiting and feeling her. She was more than any women he had ever known and he knew he was forever changed. There was and urgency to hold her, to love her. He moved slowly, savoring every second of it, she was lost in it, just as he, he had thrown back and her eyes were glazed over from his lover. She looked at him now as he moved and he never broke stride once as he laid his chest against hers and kissed her deeply. She moaned loudly, driving him more and he his pace became quicker, more demanding. Both unwilling to let go of what they felt they had moved frantically exploring and enjoying the other. She was lost in a swirling of color and heat. She felt the familiar stirrings deep down and her eyes fluttered open and she looked at him.

Her reaction was stronger than any she'd ever had before. It ripped through her and she felt it shoot through even her fingers and toes. She yelled out his name as it happened and something about that pushed him over the edge as well. He grabbed her face and leaned down over her as he found release inside her. They lay that way for a long time, both feeling and thinking. Neither of them wanting to move. She drifted off to sleep at some point and knew she was safe.

He woke up before she did and stood looking at her. She was curled on her side, oblivious to the fact she was being watched. He was lost and confused at himself. Last night he had broken more than one of his own rules. He had never been so careless with anyone. She could be pregnant from what they had done. Thinking it brought up images of what their child would look like and the warm feeling spread through him and he swore inwardly to himself. What the hell was wrong with him? He knew before he even admitted it to himself, he wanted her, wanted to be with her. She was moving, but there was no way he would allow it now. She was in his bed, and in his heart. He was all over the place with her. One minute he wanted to protect her and the next, he wanted to scold her because she was so stubborn. He wasn't sure what he would do now. He padded his way back into the living room and decided to start plating food. She would be up soon and they had to talk. This time not laying in a bed, or nothing would ever get discussed. He picked up her bag from the floor and when he did, he found a notepad with something scratched on it.

When finally she woke up, she knew he was gone. She moved to the shower and washed the lovemaking off of her from before. She felt him come in before he said a word. He waited, a hooded look to his eyes

"Why didn't you tell me someone was trying to hurt you, Sierra?" He picked up the soap from the dish and lathered up the sponge she was holding. He started with her shoulders, making lazy circles as he washed her.

"Why would I tell you, A.J.?" she managed to get the words out despite the sensations he was creating with the sponge. He moved the sponge lower lathering her as he went.

"I told you that you belong to me, Sierra, and that means everything. If anyone tries to hurt you, that is my business too."

She bit her lip to keep from giving him the satisfaction of knowing what he was doing to her again. When he was around, she lost all control of her body. He turned off the water and dried her off helping her get dressed in a shirt of his. She had to admit to herself she was left wanting more. They walked into the kitchen where the food was still warm and he played it for them all the while watching her. She looked at him, she had never seen him this way. He was wearing sweats and a t-shirt. Gone was the tailored suit and tie, even his hair was a ruffled mess, and she was lost.

"Sierra, hello." He was waving his hand in front of her and she snapped back to the present.

Finally, he asked.

"This guy, is his name Brandon? Don't lie to me."

"Yes, but how did you know that A.J.?" she stopped eating and looked at him.

"I had someone look into the situation this afternoon after you left. They are coming by tonight with an update. I'd rather you know now, than to be upset later." He took a long drink. "Then there is this." He slapped the notepad from her bag on the table and she went pale.

"A.J. it's not what you think." She took a step backwards as he turned to look at her, anger apparent on his face.

"Really, it's not?" he read from the list. "Get him to fall for me pros, Jacobs meds, great sex... thanks for that one by the way, not being scared." He looked at her with her head down now. "Cons of getting him to fall for me. He is a playboy, great sex and the best one... incapable of love." He threw the pad on the table in her direction.

"I write a lot about what's in my head, A.J. that's all. I knew better and I wouldn't even try...."

He cut her off "Really, you wouldn't try? When you first came in the office tonight you were handsy then, were you not trying?" He was bitter and upset.

"Well, yes, but I knew it was wrong and I couldn't... I'm not stupid, A.J., I knew better than to even consider it." She grabbed the pad up from the table and walked over to face him. "Exactly what part are you mad about, A.J.? The fact that I said the sex was great or the fact that someone else considered turning your own games against you, which is it?" She spun around but he was there in an instant. He was inches away from her face and his eyes softened.

"You're right, everything on that list is right, so I guess you win. I brought you here to protect you, I'm not as horrible as you think."

She was angry. "You have no right to get involved, A.J., he is misguided and yes, he scares me but this is not your problem to look into." She stood quickly and made her way back to the bedroom they had shared only hours before. She looked around gathering her clothes, but her bag was gone. She was on her way back into the kitchen where he still sat eating and she stopped. He didn't move, only continued to eat.

When she headed towards the door he finally spoke to her. "Sierra, don't."

He said it with such deep intent, it made her freeze in her tracks. He was there in an instant. He stood in front of her, between her and the door. He reached up and gently brushed her hair away from her face. She saw something different in his eyes then, something she couldn't place. He reached up and cupped her face in his hand and kissed her gently. Suddenly there was a knock on the door. He stood back and opened it, letting in a man in a dark coat. He grabbed her hand in his and brought her with him to the bar where the man could share his findings.

"This man, Brandon Baker, he isn't who he says he is. We checked your car and spoke with some people in the neighborhood and we are pretty sure he is the one who did it. That isn't the real problem."

Sierra felt the dread welling up inside her as he continued to speak. Whatever it was, it couldn't be good.

"His description fits a suspect that is wanted in the disappearance of a woman in Montana. Apparently he was too overwhelming and suddenly she went missing. The guy they are looking for is Richard Carson, but I was able to track his entrance into town around the same time Mr. Randolph disappeared from Montana. I think it's worth looking into."

A.J. spoke first. "Thank you Darius. I'll be in touch, but I definitely want this handled, and quickly."

Sierra was in shock, the tears streaming down her face. She dated Brandon for two years before he started to act this way, at any moment she could have been hurt. She had to get home where she was safe, where everyone was safe. She turned around and suddenly he was there. He pulled her into his arms and she let it all go, the tears and her heartache, for the time spent with someone who could hurt her. She pulled away and wiped her face.

"I have to go home, to my father's." She headed back to the door.

"No, it's not safe Sierra, stay here, with me." He stood there and she glanced between the door and him. She wasn't sure what to do.

"Then what, A.J., stay here until morning and then be scared to even go home to get my things?" She slumped down to the couch. She started to put on her shoes and he watched her helplessly.

She suddenly leaned forward and he knew she was crying. Instinctively he moved towards her, gathering her up in his arms. He knew she wouldn't put up a fight and he carried her to his room and his bed. She silently let the tears go unchecked down her face. She didn't want to fight the emotions anymore, she just needed to let it all go. She didn't say a word as he undressed her and tucked her into the bed. He followed suit and spooned in behind her, pulling her into his arms. She rolled over and let him wrap her up, laying her head on his chest and cried until she was asleep. He looked down at her, gently stroking her hair and enjoying the heat of her body against this. There was a simple pleasure in this, something with no sexual bearing, he was in uncharted territory. He was losing himself with her, his focus had shifted to loving her, and protecting her. She was determined to run, but he wouldn't let her, she just needed to realize what she felt back to him too. It would take some patience, but he would show her, he had too, or lose herself in the process.

Sierra was aware of everything around her. She had been lying there, thinking about what was to come for a long time. He was there, beside her. It felt like the most natural thing in the world to be here with him like this. She was in love with him, but he would never know it. He was a playboy and that would never change. She slid away from him slightly and in his sleep, he pulled her back to him. With a sigh, she let herself feel for a while longer. The next time she woke he was gone. She had planned to try and leave quietly, not disturbing him. It was no longer an option since he was in the kitchen. She threw on his shirt and walked quietly into the room and watched him. He was humming to himself and stirring something on the stove. He finally noticed her there and he froze.

Standing there, in his shirt and her hair a tangled mess she was the most beautiful thing he had ever seen. She was watching him with a half-smile and he could almost feel his heart beating out of his chest. He looked like an idiot standing there staring and he shook his head slightly to get it together.

"I see you're up, sleepyhead, coffee is ready and breakfast will be in a moment." He turned back to what he was doing and she watched the muscles in his back flex as he worked. There was something sexy about a man cooking and she smiled despite the knowing fear in her stomach about the day to come.

"Thank you, I have to go soon, but I'll stay and eat. It looks heavenly!" He delivered her eggs and bacon with pancakes and she sat back overwhelmed by the food on her plate.

"Sorry, I have a rather big appetite for breakfast food." He shrugged and joined her at the bar.

They ate in silence, neither wanting to broach the topic at hand. They would smile from time to time, but it was a quiet affair. Once everything had been cleared, she couldn't avoid it any longer.

"A.J., I can't thank you enough, for everything you did for me last night." She gave him a smile as she wound her mass of hair up into a bun.

He watched the woman he loved become the woman he was afraid of, all business and stern.

"Sierra, we need to talk. I don't want you to move, especially with that guy still running loose. I don't trust the situation." He couldn't say the words he was really feeling, not yet, it was still too new.

"It's not just about that, A.J. There is much more to it. My father needs me."

He stood. "I asked you if your family needed you, if they were in trouble." He frowned at her.

"I know you did, and I just didn't want to add to the situation, I'm sorry." She slipped out of his shirt and changed back into her clothes. He took a steadying breath as he watched her naked form move and sway with her movements, this was damn near killing him.

He moved towards her and upped her chin in his hand. "Tell me Sierra, please talk to me."

She looked at his expression and knew he was being sincere. With a sigh she settled back into the barstool. "My father is taking out a loan on the house today and I have to go sign paperwork with him. It's a legal issue more than anything. When my mother died I was given executor over the estate because my father didn't want to have any part of it, he was devastated when she died."

"Why does he need to take out a loan on the house?" He frowned.

"It doesn't matter why A.J., you asked what I had to do, and I told you." Her eyes were flashing at him and he knew she was angry. As she went into the bathroom to fix her face, he took matters into his own hands, that's how she found him when she came back out.

"Oh yes, I completely understand, yes, Mr. Ford. I'm happy to help, really, that won't be necessary. Give him a hug from us. Okay, bye."

She was standing there with her hands on her hips, fuming. When he hung up he knew there would be hell before she even began.

"Was that my father? My father, A.J., really you went to him? Since when do you have his number anyway!" she was pacing and he watched her, amused.

"Since lunch, we exchanged numbers. To be fair Sierra, I asked you first, but you wouldn't tell me anything, so I asked him." He moved towards her and she backed away and he frowned.

"You have no right always butting into everything I do, A.J., you shouldn't have called him, now he is going to worry. I dumped all of our problems at his feet, he is going to be worried. I won't be there today to handle the business side of the situation. What exactly did he tell you?" She stopped pacing and peered at him.

"You don't need to go sign the paperwork, he decided not to take a loan out on the house. We talked about Jacob, of course." He waited for the next round of anger to start.

"What did you do, A.J., what did you do?" She whispered it and he was even more concerned. He could handle her fire, but this was new.

"I took care of it, I offered to pay for Jacobs's medicine. You could have talked to me about it, Sierra. I would have helped." She flashed him a look and he felt it like a slap.

"Is that how it is now, A.J.? I stay here, we are... together and now you swoop in and fix my problems?" She waited.

He was angry now. "Hours ago Sierra, I confronted you about planning the same thing. You contemplated it and now you're throwing it at me when the fact of the matter is I'm not doing it for any other reason than the fact that I love you." He was yelling now and he watched her face shift and turn red. He ran a hand through his hair and walked to the bedroom to cool off. He knew she couldn't go anywhere and he needed to breathe, she made him crazy and he had just said he loved her. He felt her enter the room before he even saw her. He turned around to see her crying and he immediately sobered.

"Don't do that Sierra, I can't handle you crying. I am sorry, for whatever I did wrong. It doesn't change the way I feel."

"I love you too, A.J. I think I always have." She wiped her face.

He felt his heart soar as he took the few short strides to her and he gathered her up in his arms.

"Arnold." He kissed her and held her close.

"What?" She looked back up at him puzzled.

"That's what the A stands for. It's Arnold, and I thought since we love each other you should know." He gave her a smile.

"What about the J?" She waited.

"Oh no, one name at a time, you have to earn the other one." She giggled and he kissed her again.

******

The Billionaire's Caregiver

People often think a new beginning is something that happens when there is a tragedy. Shelby Watson, on the other hand, disagrees entirely. Sometimes, a new beginning can simply happen to someone, and not be some epiphany out of the ashes of what was once a mess.

Simply put, life happens, but starting over is never easy. Shelby sighed and stretched out her legs on the sofa. Tomorrow, she would start again. Never one to be defeated, she knew she could pull herself out of this "new mess" she was in.

There was something about the way her big toe poked through the worn socks that made her rethink that idea entirely.

"You and me, Dobbs...she scooped up her puppy who had buried its head under the thick blanket. "All we really need is each other." Dobbs was a Chihuahua mix. Shelby found him by the door of her apartment one day, and when she opened her apartment door, he ran right in, in front of her.

He had been there since. It may have been the forlorn look he had about him that Shelby found endearing, or just the fact that he was standing there soaked to the bone. Whatever it was, Shelby knew she couldn't leave him out there, so let him stay.

The sound of banging caused Shelby to wince slightly. The pipes in this old building were always making some awful noise whenever someone was taking a shower. Shelby looked around at her efficiency apartment.

Clean and tidy it, was her home. She lived in the 3rd block of town. The lower the number indicated the worse sections of town. This was no exception. Her neighbors all consisted of drug dealers and prostitutes, though none unfriendly. Shelby would work early mornings and try to be home before dark. As long as she kept to herself nothing bad would happen to her...well less likely to, anyway.

All of the details of her life had changed now. The part-time morning job she had been able to find, she had lost. Nothing of her doing, simply a cut in positions at the senior home she was working at. They had pulled her aside that morning and given her the bad news.

"Shelby, your work here has always been wonderful. I hope you realize this is not a reflection on the quality of your work. It's simply based on the financial needs of the company." Dr. Brenner sighed and looked over at her as he delivered the news.

"Many of the seniors are moving into better equipped facilities and they...well they already have staff there. He ran his thin bony fingers through is even thinner hair.

It was obvious to Shelby this wasn't something he enjoyed doing and decided to help take the pressure off.

"I understand Dr. Brenner. I really do. I just don't know how I'm going to make it now." Life had always been a series of ups and downs for Shelby, and this was just one more set back. She stood to stand and extended her hand to Dr. Brenner.

"Thank you for helping me get things going here Dr. Brenner. The last three years have been wonderful. I hope you will let me use you for a reference." He stood and methodically pumped her hand, covering the hands with his other one.

"I really am sorry, Shelby."

There was a sense of helplessness that Shelby felt when she headed home. Now, she and her pup gracefully sat on the old worn sofa she had gotten from the thrift store down the street. Shelby decided it was time to start sorting the factors of her life out. She jumped up and grabbed her notebook from the counter.

Determined, she created her spreadsheet, lists of bills, things to do, what not to do, etc. Balancing her checkbook, Shelby calculated that she was ok for the next three weeks, but when the rent was due, she would be in trouble. She walked into her kitchen and pulled some canned spaghetti from the cupboard, methodically putting them in a bowl and then the microwave.

This is not where she envisioned herself a few years ago. She had big plans to go back to college to get her graduate degree in nursing. She was barely scraping by, but she knew that her resilience was powerful and that she would make it through. The one thing she was sure of was that she would not cry about it but would just keep moving on.

The next day things seemed bleak. Shelby walked to the corner store and bought a newspaper and began sifting through the want ads looking for a job. She wasn't above doing anything and would do whatever necessary to keep things going. Sitting on her foot, she took notice of anything related to her field first.

Under the dark header she saw an ad for a home health nurse. Perfect. She picked up the phone and called, but was greeted by a nasty voice.

"Kayla I told you I can't do this with you right now. You will just have to trust me. It's better this way." Shelby winced at the explosion.

"I'm sorry Sir. I think I may have the wrong number, I was calling about an ad." As she began to cradle the phone back into the receiver, she heard him yell.

"Wait yes, Oh God I'm an idiot. Miss...Miss?" He was obviously flustered.

"I'm here."

"Good. I'm terribly sorry. Your number was just like someone else's, and well... Ok, so yes, can you come out today? I need to wrap this up before I leave this weekend, and I have only gotten a few responses."

Encouraged, Shelby shot up out of her chair. "Yes, of course I can, what time?"

"Um, let me think." She heard shuffling on the other end. "How about now?"

"Now?" Shelby looked around mentally, figuring out what to wear." Sure now is good. I just need an address."

After getting all the necessary information, Shelby changed into a light grey dress and black boots. Shelby pulled her hair back and gathered up all of her references. As she started to walk out, she grabbed her purse and said a silent prayer.

"Wish me luck Dobbs, this is for dinner tonight."

Maneuvering her car down the highway was easy. Shelby loved road trips and had been into the town of Fauquier many times. Often considered the "rich" area, she never had much opportunity or reason to come this far out before.

Today was different. She had an interview, and hoped it would fix this mess she was in. Pulling down the long winding road into the countryside, Shelby admired the houses as she passed them. Most of them were old, and laced with gingerbread latticework. They looked warm and cozy. At the end of one street in particular, Shelby found the house she was looking for.

All she could do was stop the car and look up in awe. There is no way, she thought to herself. The magnificent mansion was on top of a ridge high above the roadway. There was a winding back entrance that was gated, and the front lawn was landscaped perfectly. Shelby glanced over at her car with it's rusted out fenders, and wondered if she really knew what she was doing.

With a sigh, she pushed her glasses back up and drove up the driveway. She pulled off to one side, straightening her dress as she stood and shut the door. She mentally prepared herself for whatever was on the other side of the door, took a deep breath, and knocked.

Billionaire, Michael had never been more frustrated in his life. He was handling the merger of two companies, trying to line up a meeting with his partner, and simultaneously trying to find someone who could come sit with his grandmother. At 40, Michael was all business with dark hair and eyes and didn't have time for anything frivolous. His grandmother was his only soft spot. She had raised him, and her encouragement is what created the man he was now.

Suddenly ill, the doctors believed she had a stroke, and now she was in bed and unwilling to do anything. He glanced over at the clock. Where was this girl anyway? She seemed interested, but was probably another "no show." He started gathering up some paperwork just as there was a knock at the door.

Shelby waited patiently. When the door finally did open, she found herself stunned for a moment as she looked at the most handsome man she had ever met. Tall and dark, he was almost like a sculpture. Trying not to stare, she attempted to recover quickly.

"Hello, I'm Shelby. We spoke on the phone." She held out her hand to him.

Michael took her hand, shaking it lightly. He was not without his own reaction to her. Small and petite, she had hair piled on top of her head. It was dark brown and a wonderful accent to her almond-colored eyes. She wore little makeup, and was a natural beauty.

"I'm glad you're here, though I thought you would have been here sooner." Shelby frowned at the gruffness in his voice. He wasn't as pleasant as she had hoped.

"I'm sorry, I was coming from Manassas." She tried not to take offense, as he was obviously very busy.

"I see. I am looking for someone to care for my grandmother. Full-time and an occasional Saturday. I try to be here on weekends as often as I can, and she has another nurse as well. I need someone who can try to get her to do more, or at least want to. She had a stroke a month ago and the doctors think she should be fine to get out again, but she is simply laying there." He paused to look her over.

"You're very small. Are you sure this is something you'd be interested in?"

Shelby felt the anger rise. "Mr. Jameson, I can assure you that I am very capable, despite your opinion of my small stature. Would it be possible for me to meet your grandmother? I think it's always important to see how well I click with someone."

"Sure that's fine. She knows you're coming. We can head upstairs in just a few moments. I'd like to ask a few more questions first, if that's ok?"

"Certainly." Shelby relaxed slightly. The fact that this guy was an ass made the fact that he was gorgeous much easier to look past.

"Ok so I see you are working with Everest Healthcare. Do you plan to continue to do that as well?"

"If so, this may be a bad idea. I really need 100% attention for this. My grandmother is very important to me, and multitasking is something most people think they are good at, but sadly..." he looked her over once again, "are not."

Fuming, Shelby responded in clipped tones. "No, I am no longer there. I was let go recently." Before she could elaborate, Michael interjected quickly.

"Why? Was there some sort of horseplay or something? I won't tolerate any of that at all, Miss Watson. I simply won't. You do seem rather young, and I can understand if this is something that you don't feel you can handle."

He stood up as if he was dismissing her entirely.

Panic set in but even that wasn't enough to calm her anger. "Mr. Jameson, I have been working at this for a long time. I am not young, as you so nicely put it, and as a matter of fact, I'm 33. I love this type of work, and the reason I was let go was for budget cuts, not horseplay. Perhaps if you allowed people to answer your questions without simply writing them off, you would have more candidates for this position."

Shelby stood to leave.

Fire and ice. That was all he could think of. She was absolutely adorable when she was mad. He could see how her nose slightly turned red as she had been giving him a piece of her mind and although not used to being talked to like that, he gained a new kind of respect for her.

"Point taken, Miss Watson. Shall we go meet my grandmother?" He held the door to the hallway for her and allowed her to pass as he made his way up the stairs motioning for her to follow. Shelby was surprised she had even gotten this far. He was a real piece of work, this guy. Money did that to people, she thought, and could only assume that was it. Along the hallway there was artwork. Some bright, some dull, and some muted. It was a lot to take in. As they rounded the top of the stairs, Shelby looked down and couldn't help but think that her meager apartment would fit in the foyer below.

Nancy Jameson was in good spirits. She wanted to do more, but her body just wouldn't allow her to. Besides, when she is here like this, Michael comes around more. He was her only grandson and always had been her favorite.

She had three granddaughters, but they all had their own families, and were too busy to ever visit. Michael had always been special. He had dark coloring like his grandfather and was just as stubborn. She smiled warmly as Michael entered the room with a petite brunette in tow.

Nancy didn't miss the sparks that flew from the young lady's eyes as Michael made some comment on how he could show her how to use the elevator if need be.

"Grandmother this is ...I'm sorry what your name was again?" He did look guilty so Shelby took pity on him and extended her hand to Nancy.

"Hello my name is Shelby, how are you?"

"Well I'm in this bed deary so not very good, I suppose." She winked at Shelby and smiled wide.

"My grandson feels like he needs to find someone to watch over me and make me do things I am not ready to do. I suppose that's why you're here my dear. Come over here and let me get a look at you."

Having taken an immediate liking to Grandmother Nancy, Shelby complied and walked over towards the bed. Nancy noticed how her grandson followed Shelby's every move. This was interesting indeed and was exactly the distraction she needed!

After a while of discussion and rules, Shelby stood to leave. "It was very nice to meet you Miss Jameson."

"Now Dear, if you're going to be here with me all the time, I insist you call me Nancy or Grandmother, whatever suits you."

"Grandmother, no one has offered Miss Watson a job yet. I hardly think she needs to start calling you Grandmother." Michael chuckled.

"Michael Dear, it is my money is it not?" Grandmother smiled up at him lovingly and patted his hand on the bed. "So, I say she is hired."

"Shelby that is if you will take the job of course."

Never a person to have nothing to say, it took everything Shelby had not to laugh at the interplay. It would seem that Grandmother Nancy was the only one to bring Michael down a peg or two. If for that reason alone, Shelby would take the job.

"I would love to Nancy." Shelby smiled up at Nancy and then at Michael.

There was some mix of being irritated by his grandmother's words and being floored by the smile that Shelby gave him. He didn't know what to say. After clearing his throat, he kissed his grandmother on the head and turned to leave.

"Miss Watson, if you will kindly follow me back down stairs, we can go over pay and hours, and so on."

Shelby said her goodbyes again and followed Michael down the stairs. He even smelled good, like leather and soap. What was most adorable was the way his hair curled in the back of his neck just slightly. What in the world was wrong with her?

Never suckered in by the connection between men and women, she usually had a fairly good grasp on self-control. Sure she had met a few nice guys and done her share of dating, but that was a long time ago and there had been no one in at least three years. Maybe that was it, she needed to get out more.

Offering her a chair, Michael detailed the terms and pay of the job. More money than she could imagine, Shelby sat stunned while he rambled on.

"Miss Watson is that acceptable?" She glanced up at him sharply. Oh no, what had she missed.

"Yes of course, that's more than fair."

"When can you start?" He watched her closely. He could almost watch the play of emotions she was thinking and feeling.

"Anytime is fine. I don't live far, even if I was late today. So I am free anytime."

"I'm not sure if you realize that this job is more than just being here from one time to another. Obviously, you will have to move in here, as that is part of the deal." He moved to gather up his things and glanced at his watch. He was already late and was starting to get irritated, as this matter should have been handled over an hour ago.

"Oh no, I can't do that Mr. Jameson, I have my own place. I'll stay there." He was surprised. He had seen the worn shoes she was wearing, and heard the racket her poor car made as it climbed the hill to the house. He just assumed that she would be more than happy to move in.

"Suit yourself, but I may need you sleep over on occasion. Is that fair?" He caught her eye again and reached out to shake her hand.

He was all business and it suited him. She reached out and felt the warmth as he took her hand in his. She felt like he lingered perhaps just a second longer than normal; but it was probably just her imagination. There was something powerful about the way he carried himself. Like right now, just staring at her. Closing her eyes for a moment, she managed to get out "Of course."

After saying their goodbyes, Shelby made her way to the car and headed home. What was it about Michael Jameson that made her crazy? He was arrogant, stubborn and bossy. He was also handsome, loving to his grandmother, and made her feel safe. All of that from one visit. Thankfully, he didn't live in the house year round, or she would be in trouble for sure.

The next few months were a flurry of activity. Shelby commuted every day to her job with Nancy which she loved, and had enough money to pay up her rent for a while. Michael and she spoke on the phone almost every day discussing Grandmother's day and how things were going. He typically had a joke to tell, but on some days, he was distant and moody.

Either way, they had come a long way and she considered him a friend. Gone was the canned spaghetti, and Shelby was actually able to cook food for herself. Even Dobbs was happier. She had just settled down to watch TV for a bit before turning in when the phone rang. It was a frantic Michael.

"Watson, my grandmother seems to have had a heart situation of some kind. I am in town and headed to the hospital and she has asked to see you." He was obviously in pain as he choked it out. Despite their differences, Michael had been nothing but nice with her and she didn't want to see him hurt. Worry was a motivator for Shelby and she immediately started to change clothes as he talked.

"..wanted to know if she had been acting differently lately or anything?"

"NO no she's been fine, and we have actually been walking a few times and..."

He cut her off immediately. "You had her walking? What in the world, Watson were you thinking? She wasn't ready for that. Just come to the hospital as soon as you can." He hung up leaving Shelby stunned.

She was frustrated herself wondering if he was right. She gathered up her purse and headed downstairs. Trying to avoid the people in the halls, she made it to her car safely and let out a deep sigh. Unfortunately, it was not meant to be. As she turned the key nothing happened. Slowly, she laid her head on the steering wheel. What now? She jumped out to look under the hood. Apparently, sometime during the night, someone had stolen her battery… now she was stuck. Knowing she could never forgive herself if she didn't see Nancy, Shelby made her way back to her apartment and called him.

"Yes What!" He yelled into the phone.

"Michael, please don't yell at me."

"Oh it's you. I'm sorry, Watson. The number thing again. Yes what's up?"

After much explaining, it was settled that Michael would come by and pick Shelby up on his way. She wasn't too far from the hospital herself but at night it was better to ride with someone. A few minutes later Shelby heard the knock on her door and opened it to a disheveled Michael. He was a mess, worry etched on his face, but handsome as ever.

Michael took in the apartment, if that's what you call it. Small but tidy, he imagined she could do just about everything. His issue was with her neighbors.

"This..is where you live, Shelby?" He gestured to the occupants sitting in the halls and the loud music.

"Yes why?" Shelby had her pride. This was her place and it wouldn't sit well if he was insulting.

"I'm terrified for my safety out there. I can't imagine how you've made it all this time. You're so small and there are at least 20 people just hanging outside."

"I am not so small and I am just fine. Let's go." She crammed her gloves into her purse and yanked open the door leaving it open so he could follow.

In the car Michael looked over at her. She had her signature bun in place and there was a pained look on her face. Obviously, he had hurt her feelings.

"Look Watson, I'm sorry. I didn't mean anything by it. I just worry. I mean grandmother worries about you is all." She had noticed the slip he made and smiled inwardly. He cared.

They arrived at the hospital and Nancy looked tired, but was noticeably happy to see her two favorite people. These two sure move slowly and I'm not getting any younger, she thought. She smiled at them both. What a striking couple they make. This little heart "issue" was just what was needed to bring them together for a while.

"Oh my dears, I'm so happy to see you both. They say I'm ok but are keeping me for a few days for observation. Can you imagine two whole days? I'll be bored out of my mind." Truthfully, she was glad. She had been feeling uncomfortable today but she knew Michael was coming to town and wanted he and Shelby to spend some time together.

"I'm just glad you're ok." Shelby was concerned at how pale she was. "This is my fault. We shouldn't have been walking this week."

"Oh pish posh. It's probably just gas or something." Michael rolled his eyes at his grandmother.

It was at that time that the nurse came in.

"I'm sorry, but you'll both have to get going Mrs. Jameson need to rest..."

They said their goodbyes and headed out front. Michael was very quiet, brooding again over some business merger gone wrong or something. She glanced over at him and he was caught up in thought, so she let the ride continue on in silence.

They pulled into her apartment complex and Shelby began to open the door.

"Wait, Watson I'm going up with you. I need to make sure you get in there in one piece."

"You don't have to do that Michael, I'm fine." She started walking and he followed anyway.

As they reached the top stairs of the building, a man reached over and touched Shelby on her leg making her jump. Michael immediately jumped.

"Don't touch her!" he moved between Shelby and the man.

"Michael it's fine. He is harmless." Secretly, she was touched that he jumped to her rescue.

Opening the door, they went inside. Michael was again impressed by the simple charm of her place. He sat down on the sofa and was greeted by a flying ball of fur. "Oh my, what is this?" He scruffed the dog on the back of the head and it bounced off.

"You once told me you had a dog but I hardly think that little thing qualifies, Watson." He smiled up at her.

Shelby had moved to the other end of the couch. "He is something, that's for sure." She giggled as they watched him get into a fight with a dog toy.

"You should just move into the house with us, Shelby." Hearing these words, Shelby caught her breath. She even noticed he had used her first name.

"Why would I do that? I'm perfectly fine here." What she didn't say was that she couldn't handle watching him with the various women he dated. She cared too much about Grandmother Nancy to ruin her relationship by being too close to him."

At that moment there was an obvious gunshot. Michael jumped up, and in his demanding voice she had grown to love he simply stated, "Get some things, Watson you're going with me."

The ride to the house was uneventful. Shelby knew he was mad, but to be honest, she wasn't sure why. He parked his car in front of the house and they went inside together. "You can have the room down here. I'll sleep upstairs and you know your way around. I'm getting a drink, I certainly need it."

She could use one herself, she thought as she went into the spare room downstairs. Changing into pajamas, letting her hair down, and tucking Dobbs into the bed, Shelby decided to go into the den where Michael was and get that drink. If, for any other reason but to calm her nerves. Knowing they were here alone was setting her on edge.

He was sitting in the leather-bound chair by the fireplace. He already had a drink, or was it two? Nothing could prepare him for her entrance. It felt like someone had punched him in the stomach. She was in all pink and her hair was flowing down her back. This casual image of her was one he had played out in his mind during one of their conversations on the phone. He had thought about it ...and now here it was.

He watched her walk over to the bar, pour a drink for herself, and tip it back. Impressive he thought. He stood up and moved closer to her. He could see all the shades of auburn in her hair when he was up close like this, she smelled like honeysuckle.

"You're moving in here, Watson." He said it with a finality that only made her angry.

"You can't tell me what to do, Michael. I work for you, but you don't own me." She was flushed with anger as he turned towards her.

"You could be killed, Watson. That place is dangerous, men groping you in the halls and gunshot...real actual gunshot, Watson." He ran his hand though his hair.

"My grandmother would kill me if anything happened to you and I didn't try and stop it." She couldn't help but feel some disappointment at the words. She had hoped he would say something about how he cared.

"I'm not moving in Michael. Let it go." She put her glass down and turned to leave. He grabbed her left arm and spun her around. It could have been the alcohol or the stress of the day, but something made him lose himself in that moment.

He gripped her wrist tighter than he meant to and put his right hand into the waves of her hair, pulling her towards him. The kiss had meant to be angry. He needed her to listen to reason but what started out hard, became softer, deeper, and more meaningful. Slowly, he dropped her other wrist and cupped her face in his hands, nipping at her lips and taking in the smell of her skin. When the kiss broke, he looked up at her.

"Watson, you're driving me crazy." He dropped his hands back down and watched the emotions play out on her face. Rocked to her core, Shelby could only stand and wait. Wait for the fluttering to subside, wait for her heart to stop racing, and wait for him to stop looking at her so intently. Not knowing what to say, she turned and walked stiffly back into her room. He followed her.

"Talk to me Watson. Why are you running from me? I know you feel this craziness just like I do."

"Yes I do Michael and that's why I won't live here." She turned to look at him. "I am a mess inside and I need you to go and leave me be so I can think straight." She saw the pained look on his face but heard him leave the room.

Shelby laid in bed thinking about that kiss. His kiss only intensified the connection they had. It wasn't all her. That was comforting, but what wasn't, was that she couldn't stop the fluttering she felt deep down. The way he moved towards her and the way he kissed deeply and without thought.

Laying here was obviously not going to figure it all out. She decided to go get a drink of water. They came from such different worlds. He always had someone worldly on his arm, some debutante. She had even met a few of them when he was there and she had been working.

The one thing they all had in common was that they were beautiful. Always regal and gorgeous, she always found something to do to keep away from them. After they would leave, Grandmother Nancy always had some snide comment about each one that made Shelby giggle.

"He will never find the right one unless he shops from a different field," she would say. Smiling now, Shelby opened the refrigerator door and started sifting through things until she found exactly what she wanted. Cake, it was the best cake around and had been left over from a party Grandmother Nancy had earlier that week. She stood there eating quietly, not hearing him until he spoke.

"You have quite the "strictly business" thing going on here, Watson."

She slammed the door shut on impulse, having been caught red handed.

"Yeah I try." She smiled slightly. He walked over to her and with one finger, wiped the chocolate off her bottom lip.

Feeling the heat begin to creep up again, Shelby took a step back.

"We need to talk Watson, and now." He walked until she had backed up to the bar. He moved his face closer to hers.

"I think it's obvious that I want you. I don't know how else to put it." The bluntness of the statement made Shelby gasp.

"The only way I'm going to stop trying is if you tell me you don't feel the same way." She was pinned between him and the bar and he was watching her face.

"Michael let me go," she tried to squirm but it was no use. She was stuck.

"Just tell me you don't want me to touch you and I'll leave you alone Watson. Just say it."

Knowing full well she felt the same way he did she, Shelby did the only thing she thought was right. She looked up at him and ran her finger down the right side of his face.

"I can't tell you any of that, Michael because I want the same thing." Before she could finish the words, he crushed his mouth to hers. He put his hands in her hair tilting her head back more. She kissed him back more fervently, having let go now. He lifted her up off the floor and put her on the bar top. Running his hands along her legs, all the while teasing and nipping her bottom lip.

"We should stop Michael." It was more of a pant than a statement.

"You're right, Watson, we should, but I can't. Not anymore." Pulling her to him, he lifted and carried her into the bedroom and kicked the door shut behind him. Sitting her down, she stood motionless, watching him take his shirt off and move towards her. She was frozen to the spot she stood on, not knowing what to do next.

He walked to her and started slowly unbuttoning the front of her pajamas. Each button exposed new skin that he had to kiss. He loved the way she smelled of sunshine and honeysuckle. He looked up at her.

Needing no words, she walked backwards towards the bed, pulling him with her as they went. Sliding back onto the comforter, he followed, pressing the length of him against her body. He looked down and knew in that moment, he was lost. Her hair spilled across the pillow, her lips were parted slightly from being thoroughly kissed, and her eyes were shining up at him. He could tell she was scared and excited. He ran his finger along her bottom lip.

"I need to hear you say it, Shelby. I need us to be real in this moment and together."

He gazed at her. "I can stop if you want, but you need to tell me now before I can't anymore." His honestly made her want him even more. She slowly pulled her shirt off and tossed it to the floor.

"I want you Michael, I always have." Needing no further encouragement, Michael stood and took off the rest of his clothes looking down. He stood back for a moment, letting himself take in her naked form. She was perfect.

Once, he thought her tiny, but looking at her now, he could see every curve she was given. Almost scared to touch her, she made the move first.

"I'm getting a little self-conscious Michael. What's wrong with me?" She started to cover up again.

"No don't "...he grabbed her hand. "You're beautiful, Watson, absolutely beautiful." He laid down on the bed again, taking a moment to calm his racing heart. He was acting like a teenage school boy, wondering why in the world was so nervous.

This was different. He knew it and probably always had, but he needed her to feel loved, wanted, and cherished.

The night progressed, and the two made love into the early hours of dawn. Before falling asleep, the last thing she heard was him saying her name and draping one arm across her body. Sometime during the night, Shelby got cold, having been woken up by something, only to find herself naked as the day she was born. She tried to keep from moving, but right before she almost fell asleep, she felt Michael's arm grasp her stomach and pull her into him. He kissed her ear and they drifted back to sleep for a few more hours.

Never a late sleeper, Michael woke up to greet the day with a smile on his face. Shelby was amazing. She was not just beautiful, she was the type of woman men dream of. She gave as much as she received, and never held back. This was something Michael couldn't help but admire. He looked at her lying among the sheets as he headed upstairs to shower and get ready for the day. He just didn't have the heart to wake her up.

Shelby woke up to the smells of coffee and the clink of pans. She rolled over to snuggle in more and her eyes flew open as she remembered...everything. Oh wow she had never been so careless in her life. She scrambled to jump in the shower before he found her. Before she was soaped up she heard him come into the bathroom.

"Watson, I see you're joining me today finally." He chuckled.

"Michael really, I am in the shower, I'll be right out." She could only smile as she heard him hum a tune as he left.

What would she do now? It had happened and there was no going back, but she could stop it now. Now that they had gotten it out of their system, she could put Michael Jameson out of her mind altogether.

She entered the kitchen, dressed for the day and ready to go to the hospital. Michael was cheery and leaned towards her as if to get a kiss. She managed to avoid it discretely.

Frowning, Michael went back to cooking. Something was wrong. Breakfast passed with no mishaps and they set off for the hospital.

Grandmother was overjoyed to see them. They each took a side and listened to her tell them about how awful the night had been and the bed situation. She moved on to complain about the food and how happy she would be at home. She could tell something was amiss between the couple, but it would sort itself out.

Michael was having a hard time understanding what Shelby was thinking. The night had been something people only dream about and yet when he got close to her, she ran. Something wasn't right, but he would find out soon enough.

The doctors came in and discussed the grandmother's situation. They equated it to a chemical reaction to something she ate, at which grandmother smiled. They passed the morning laughing with her, planning the next event. At lunch, the doctors ordered them out, saying she needed her rest, so the couple decided to go to a nearby restaurant for something to eat.

It was a beautiful café, overlooking a pond and situated amongst lush landscaping. They dined on wine and oysters, which were new to Shelby. Michael was about to broach the subject plaguing him, when a woman came up to the table.

"Michael darling, where have you been?" The woman was like something from the cover of a magazine. She had on long flowing pants and a silk shirt complete with a huge brimmed hat.

"Baby, I have missed you so much. How nice of you to bring the maid to lunch." She smiled over at Shelby, who immediately excused herself and went outside.

Angry Michael pushed the woman back away from him. "I told you to leave me alone. Why are you here? Stop calling me and stop following me."

Without waiting for an answer, he stormed out onto the street and to his car. Shelby was standing by the passenger side and he opened the door, then went to his side and got in.

"I'm sorry, Watson that was ...the number..." at her confused look he added "remember when you would call and I thought it was her?"

"Aha, that is her." Shelby still felt awful about the exchange and self-conscious as well. The maid, really?

When they arrived at the house, Shelby went to her room. Thinking she would have some time to think, she was surprised when Michael stormed in behind her.

"What the hell Shelby, after last night I thought,"

"What...you thought we would just act like nothing happened? You think I would go away? Well I'm not. I love Grandmother Nancy and I'm not going anywhere."

"What are you talking about Shelby? I don't want you to go anywhere. I want you here. With me." He said it with such finality, Shelby could do no more than look up at him.

"What?"

"I love you Shelby. I have since the day we met and you came here. But when I was at your place and heard that gunshot it was all I could do to not kidnap you myself and tie you up here so I could keep you safe."

"But I'm not like you Michael. She called me "the maid" for goodness sake." She looked down for a moment.

"Shelby do you really think I care one moment about what people think?" I want you and I choose you."

Tears were flowing freely now as Shelby looked up at him.

"Well," He asked impatiently.

"Well what? " She was confused.

"Damn it Shelby, you're killing me. Do you or do you not feel anything for me?"

Laughing, she ran into his arms and kissed him. "Michael I have loved you from the moment you opened that door."

He let out an audible sigh. Happy and content, he pulled her close to him and kissed her deeply.

Hand in hand they headed back to the hospital. Grandmother had taken a nap and was refreshed as she looked out the windows to the parking lot. Seeing Michael, she smiled. He really was a good boy. But what made her happiest was seeing him hand in hand with Shelby.

Perhaps her plan had worked after all, and if she played it just right, she could somehow start planning a Fall wedding at the house. She may be getting old, but this was enough to keep her busy for at least a good many years to come.

The Billionaire's Romance

When Kate found out that her boyfriend, Ben was cheating on her, she was devastated. To make matters worse, the woman Ben was cheating with was one of Kate's best friends. "It just happened," explained Ben when Kate asked him why he was cheating on her with Caroline.

Kate loved Ben so much that she was willing to forgive his indiscretions, however, he wasn't interested. "Please don't break up with me," she cried. "I'll do anything to keep you." Ben simply wasn't in love with Kate anymore because he was falling for Caroline.

Ben and Kate continued seeing each other for another couple of months, however, the relationship was strained and it lacked intimacy and love. When they broke it off, Kate fell into a deep depression.

She couldn't eat or sleep, and it took every ounce of determination she had just to get out of bed in the morning. She worried that she would lose her job because she frequently called in due to her severe depression.

Instead of trying to focus on the positive things in her life, Kate found herself obsessed with Ben and his new girlfriend, Caroline. Kate started driving past Ben's house every night to see if Caroline was there, and she even started following him to see where he was going.

On one occasion, Kate tracked the couple down to a local restaurant. She was even so bold as to walk into the establishment and talk to Ben when Caroline got up to go to the bathroom. "What the hell are you doing here?" Ben asked. "Please talk to me," Kate begged. Ben replied, "I told you we were finished. I don't love you anymore and I'm not interested in trying to resurrect a dead relationship."

Kate was so beside herself, she didn't know how she could go on. With an important business meeting the next morning that she had to contend with, her anxiety was through the roof. She pretty much gave up on the idea of ever getting married, let alone having kids.

Kate had always struggled financially, but when she met Ben, she thought that he might be her ticket out of debt. Even though she loved him deeply, she couldn't help be attracted to his keen sense of managing money and investing. After the couple broke up, Kate dated a string of losers who weren't capable of giving her the love and support that she needed.

Kate was starting to resign herself to the single life, and was beginning to get comfortable with the idea that she might end up being a spinster like her aunt and cousin. Her breakup with Ben left her emotionally scarred with little enthusiasm to ever date again.

Things took a dramatic turn, when one day, a strikingly handsome and very wealthy man was hired at her job to replace the CEO who recently left to pursue other ventures. He was billionaire, Ashton Smith, and to Kate's delight, he wasn't wearing a wedding ring.

All this excitement quickly diverted her mind from Ben, and she was even starting to forget that he even existed. While his cheating with her friend Caroline still stung, Kate was finally starting to feel twinges of excitement when she thought about other men, especially Ashton Smith. She'd never met a billionaire before, but soon found out that he was a down-to-earth as they came.

"Hello, Kate, I'm Ashton," he said, when he greeted her on the first day they met. "It's very nice to meet you, Sir," Kate replied. "Now there won't be any of that "Sir" stuff around here," Ashton said. He was about ten years older than Kate and graduated from an Ivy League school. To say that Kate was intimidated by him was an understatement, but because of his warm demeanor, she was starting to feel comfortable around him.

The other women who worked at the company were head-over-heels in love with their new CEO, however, he didn't seem interested in any of them. Ashton treated all the employees with respect, but Kate couldn't help but feel that he gave her more attention than he did everyone else.

One evening when Kate and a few others were working late, Ashton knocked on her office door to ask if he could speak with her. Her heart began pounding and she feared that she might make a fool of herself because of her excitement. Ashton first asked about the project she was working on but the conversation soon took on a personal flavor. "Are you married?" Ashton asked. "No, but I recently broke up with my boyfriend of four years," she answered. "I'm sorry, Kate, was it a painful breakup?"

At first, Kate hesitate to divulge the sordid details of her and Ben's demise, but she reasoned that if she told Ashton about it, it might bring them closer together. "How could he cheat on you?" You are one of the most beautiful women I've ever met in my life," he said. Kate was flattered, but as soon as he said that, her "BS" meter registered off the charts.

Ashton told Kate that he too just got out of a long-term relationship with a woman he dated since college. Although they never got married, they lived together for years. He liked the idea of having someone to come home to, but never took the next step to make it legal.

Since he was getting older, Ashton was considering marriage more and more. He wanted to be in love, to feel that spark of romance, which had long disappeared from the relationship he had with his last girlfriend. Although they were together for eight years, they stopped sleeping together after the first year.

Ashton told Kate he didn't know why they stayed together for so long, especially since they only had sex a couple times a year. The relationship was a matter of convenience, really. He had an attractive woman on his arm to accompany him to his social events and she literally did everything for him.

She cooked, cleaned, did his laundry and ran his errands. Ashton was treated like a king, however, he was bored with the whole thing. Instead of ending the relationship when their passion soured after the first year, he dragged it on until he couldn't take it anymore. His girlfriend, Savannah was shocked when Ashton broke up with her. In fact, she started stalking him. While Kate "quasi" stalked Ben for about a week, she quickly got tired of it and realized the errors of her ways.

After talking about their respective relationships for about an hour, Ashton felt comfortable enough to ask Kate out for dinner. "Would you consider having dinner with me?" he asked. Kate was surprised at his tone because it almost sounded as though he was nervous. Could it have been an act in an attempt to show Kate his "humble" side?

Kate couldn't believe her luck. Not did her new gorgeous boss ask her out, he truly seemed interested in starting a relationship with her. "Oh my gosh, Jen, I have to buy a new outfit for my date but I'm so strapped for cash!" "I'd help you out, Kate, but I'm in the same boat as you," Kate's friend, Jen replied.

Because neither women had any money to fund a new dress for Kate's dinner date, she'd have to make do with what she had in her closet. She settled on a little black dress with a plunging neckline that was backless. To accentuate her ample breasts, Kate wore a long gold mesh chain that dropped nicely into her cleavage.

As 7:00 approached, Kate felt a knot in her stomach. She wondered how Ashton would look, but more importantly, she wondered how he would think she looked in her classic black dress. While not usually materialistic, Kate couldn't also help wonder what kind of car her boss would roll up in. She wouldn't have to wait long to find out because in a few minutes, her doorbell rang.

Instead of Ashton, Kate opened the door to a driver, fully decked out in a chauffeur's hat and white gloves. How nice, she thought, that Ashton hired a limo to pick her up. What she didn't know was that Ashton hadn't hired a limo. The chauffeur who came to Kate's door was Ashton's private driver who squired him around town in his brand new Bentley. Where did he get all this money, Kate wondered.

Was he born with a silver spoon in his mouth or was he a "trust fund" baby? He was a financial expert, which is why the company Kate worked for hired him as the CEO on a temporary basis to help bring the business back into the black.

During dinner, Kate found out a few more interesting tidbits about her boss and was so excited at the prospect of being his new girlfriend. It seemed as though Ashton was pushing for a relationship, and while Kate was flattered, she was taken aback. What was the rush, she wondered.

Through the grapevine, Kate found out something that disturbed her. Ashton's great uncle was nearing 100 years old, and Ashton was the only heir to his will. To further complicate matters, the uncle was in poor health and he wasn't expected to live out the year.

One of the stipulations in his will was that Ashton be married by time the will was read. If he wasn't married, the uncle's entire estate, which was worth almost a billion dollars, would be dispersed among a number of charitable organizations in which he was associated with. Since Ashton didn't want to miss out on his inheritance, he was on a mad quest to find himself a wife, fast.

Even without the money from the will, Ashton still was financially secure, but bad investments and his lavish lifestyle were quickly depleting his bank account. If he didn't find other sources of revenue, he feared that he would soon be bankrupt. He had to get married soon or else his financial future would be in jeopardy.

"How would you like to acompany me to the symphony?" Ashton asked Kate. Ordinarily, Kate would have been ecstatic, but in light of her new revelation about his uncle's will, she was hesitant to accept his offer. After giving it some more thought, Kate came to a conclusion. She thought to herself, "so what if he wants to marry me because of the will." She reasoned that they would eventually fall in love and eventually live happily ever after.

Kate envisioned herself living in a mansion, driving expensive cars, drinking fine wine and jet-setting to exotic locations. She longed for financial security ever since she was very young. Growing up poor was hard for her and even harder for her parents.

Kate vowed that if she ever "married rich," she would give her parents enough money so that their lives would change for the better. She would pay all their bills, buy them a new home and make sure that they never worried about money again.

Kate had a fantasy about she and Ashton that she replayed in her mind over and over:

Ashton shook his head moving closer to her and putting his hands on her blouse. "We're being irrational. Just go for it. He ripped the shirt from her body and it fell to the floor. His lips went to her neck, while her hands went to his shirt, removing it from the confinement of his dress pants.

She started off tediously undoing button after button, but then knew that she needed to move the show on the road. She busted open his shirt, the way that he had busted open hers.

Her hands trailed down his chest, while he continued to kiss her neck. She arched her back, sighing against his kisses. His hands went behind her back, as he slowly removed her bra. Her breasts pressed hard against his bare chest.

Her hands went to his pants and she quickly removed it from him. They fell to the floor and he kicked them off. Then his hands went to his boxers and she drug them down his legs, while his hands tweaked her nipples.

His hands slowly slid down her stomach and then wrapped around her back. He undid the zipper to her skirt and it fell to the floor.

His hands went to her panties and he looped his fingers through them, tugging them off of her body. Before she had time to comprehend the next move, she felt him lifting her into his arms and laying her down on the floor.

Their lips met, his tongue dipping inside her mouth. As their tongues clashed together, his hands continued to massage her breasts, gently feeling each part of her sensitive skin.

As his manhood was about to enter her, he pulled back. "Damn, I don't have a condom," he groaned, starting to regress.

She wrapped her arms around him and pulled him closer to her. "I'm on the pill," she whispered, as their lips met. "Ugh..." she groaned, arching her back, but not breaking from the kiss.

With each thrust, she was forced to part from the kiss. "Ugh...Oh God...yes..." she whimpered, barely able to get the words out, it felt so good.

As one arm continued being wrapped around him, her other arm fell down to her side and she tried desperately to grab anything to hold onto, finally choosing for a leg to his chair. Her hips bucked against his.

He crashed against her, with a hunger that she never endured. "Oh God...yes...yes..." he cried, pressing harder to her core. "Ugh...ugh..." he groaned, digging deeper. She could feel his pulsating manhood within her. "Damn..." he cried out.

"Ugh...ugh...yes...God yes..." she moaned, as her body seized over him. She sighed, unable to move, as his gyrations slowly began to come to an end.

"Wow..." she sighed, closing her eyes and just lying there. As she was focusing on her next move, she felt hands on her legs, parting her ever so softly.

She didn't know what he was doing, because of her inability to see straight, but she felt the entrance his finger, as it dipped inside of her. She moaned, taking in his sensual moves.

Then it was over and she was fighting disappointment, until she felt something else. She tried to control her breathing, as she felt his tongue licking every inch of her body.

"Oh God..." she whispered, but bit back a guttural groan. His tongue eased inside of her, and her eyes opened, staring at the ceiling of his office. She reached down and grabbed his head, holding him closer to her. "Yes..." she groaned, as he tenderly caressed her again.

She felt the smoothness of his moves and she sighed against his deep and masculine movements. "Hm...hmmm...hm..." she signed, her body gliding against the intensity.

As his tongue was seeking out each crevice that she could provide, she felt her body begin to shake with desire.

As his tongue slowly weaved its way out of her, she dropped her hands from his head. She closed her eyes and took in deep and slow breaths. She felt him easing his way back up her. Her eyes opened and she stared at him. She only saw desire and nothing else.

He wrapped his hand around her neck and pulled her into a breathless kiss. His tongue circling around hers. He pulled from the kiss, bringing his mouth down to her flesh of her neck. She could barely keep up, as she was fighting exhaustion.

She closed her eyes and tried to focus on his intimate paths around her skin. Between kisses, she heard his words. "You are so sexy!" She could relish in that forever.

When she felt him retracting, she heaved a sigh. He fell off of her and she could hear the restlessness that he felt. "Wow..." he mumbled, as they both just laid there and tried to catch their breath.

Kate didn't want to bring up the uncle's will with Ashton, but she hoped that he would "come clean" and tell her about it. She was actually excited about the prospect of marrying a billionaire because she knew it would benefit so many people, especially those less fortunate in her immediate family.

When Ashton picked Kate up for the symphony, he told her that he needed to talk to her about something. "I have something to tell you," he said.

"I'm starting to fall in love with you and that's why I want to be perfectly honest," Asthon explained. "You see, Kate, my uncle is very wealthy, very old, and unfortunately very sick," he explained.

"I recently found out that I am the sole heir of his will, however, I won't see a penny of his money unless I'm married at the time of the reading of the will," he said.

Kate, didn't know how to respond, but she was flattered that he told her. She found herself falling more and more in love with Ashton, and even though the couple haven't known each other for very long, she felt that they had a good foundation in which to build a strong relationship.

Ashton didn't have a lot of time to waste on courting a women because his uncle could die any day, and if this were to happen, the money would be distributed among a variety of charities.

After a long discussion, Kate and Ashton decided they wanted to pursue a long-term relationship and ultimately got engaged. The engagement lasted exactly one week because eight days after Ashton slipped a huge diamond on Kate's finger, they got married in Las Vegas.

The newlyweds made their home in Flordia, in an enormous Spanish-style mansion close to other CEOs and celebrities. While Kate enjoyed cooking for her new husband, most of their meals were prepared by private chefs. To say that Kate was spoiled by her new found wealth is an understatement.

While she was grateful that she was able to help her family financially as well as live a lifestyle that she could have only dreamed of, something was missing. Ashton was becoming distant and quiet, and although the two were still intimate, Ashton was starting to make excuses for why he didn't want to have sex. "I'm so tired, babe. I need to get a good night's sleep because I have an early business meeting in the morning," Ashton told Kate when she wanted to have sex with him.

Kate started suggesting that she and Ashton schedule "date" nights. The idea would be that they both clear their schedules on the agreed upon night so that they could enjoy each other for a few hours. Ashton seemed to like the idea, but every time the scheduled date approached, he would be full of excuses again. Kate was starting to get discouraged and questioned her decision to marry Ashton.

Kate no longer worked at the company where she met Ashton, but she kept in touch with many of the employees there. Ashton didn't work there anymore either as he was only hired on a temporary basis to help improve increase revenue.

Everyone at the office heard about Kate and Ashton's marriage and they eagerly waited for Kate to spill the details. While she talked about their prosperous life together, she never told them why they got married so quickly.

Whenever Kate came on to her husband, he retreated into a dark, sullen mood. He always felt bad about it and to make up for his lack of affection he always gifted his wife with an expensive bauble.

Kate, growing tired of her husband's distance decided to explore the famous nightlife of Florida's elite. Since she hadn't made many friends yet, she ventured out on her own one evening when Ashton was "out of town." She discovered a very active nightclub where you had to wait in line for an hour before you got in. Every one in line looked like they just stepped out of a fashion magazine and the men were incredibly good-looking.

While scoping out the people in line, she saw someone who looked very familiar. Upon closer inspection, she discovered that the person in line was Ashton. Her first instinct was to run up to him and ask him what the hell he was doing there.

After calming herself, she decided to play it cool and watch what he would do next. It seemed as though he was flirting with every woman in line, and as Kate saw it, even some of the men. Was he living a secret life? Is he attracted to both men and women? Kate didn't have any qualms of bisexuality, but she did have a problem with it when it came to her husband. If he liked men, why was he so attracted to her? Was it all a charade?

Kate was shocked when she saw Ashton slip his hand into another man's hand while waiting to gain entry into the nightclub. She felt sick to her stomach but she knew she would have to follow him in to see who this other guy was.

By this time, Kate was certain that Ashton used her to get his uncle's money, but time would only tell. Maybe he was just stressed out and was looking for an outlet to help him forget about his responsibilities.

Inside the nightclub, Kate was shocked when Ashton and the guy he was holding hands with started dancing. Ashton showed no interested in the women in the club, and he seemed to be in his own little world with his new "friend." This was Kate's husband, and she felt betrayed. She was devastated and demoralized, and instead of ignoring the situation hoping it would go away, she boldly approached Ashton on the dance floor.

"What the hell is going on, Ashton?" Kate asked. Ashton could have been knocked over with a feather. He was in total shock, as was his companion. "Kate, what are you doing here?" Ashton replied. "I'd like you to meet an old friend of mine, Rick."

"Ashton, cut the crap," Kate said. "Do you think I'm stupid?"

"I saw you two holding hands and acting like a couple on the dance floor," she said.

"Rick, did you know that Ashton is married?" Rick had no idea that Ashton was married, but for some reason, it didn't seem to bother him.

Kate started thinking about Ashton's uncle's will. She believed that Ashton married her under false pretenses. Sure, he seemed like he was into her when they made love, but could it have all been an act? Was he thinking about a man the whole time?

It all started adding up. Ashton was making excuses to avoid intimacy with Kate because he was gay. He simply wasn't attracted to her and the only reason he proposed was to get his uncle's multi-billion dollar fortune.

Kate was furious about the deceit and vowed to reveal his secret to the executor of the will. She didn't care about living in the lap of luxury. While she knew that Ashton was in a rush to get married, she assumed that they would grow to love one another, and certainly, she thought her future husband was heterosexual. Had she known he was gay, she would never have married him, money or no money.

Kate wishes she never met Ashton and feels she was worse off after getting married than she was before. The only good thing about this marriage, according to Kate, was that she was able to financially help her family so that they could live a better life. The marriage was void of any love and affection, and now, it was based on lies and deceit.

Kate discovered who the executor of Ashton's uncle will was and decided to contact him. She was nervous when she dialed his number, but knew it was the right thing to do. Not only because Ashton had deceived her, but because he tainted his uncle's dying wish by marrying under false pretenses so that he could acquire the multi-billion dollar fortune.

When the executor of the will answered the phone, who incidentally was a long-time trusted business associate of the uncle, Kate introduced herself and began to tell her story. The executor, Blaine Daniels, seemed uninterested at first, but as Kate further detailed her relationship with Ashton, he was intrigued.

Blaine, an attorney, deemed that Ashton indeed got the estate under false pretenses and vowed to take legal action against him. While it might take months or even years to prove that Ashton got married for the sole purpose of acquiring the fortune, Blaine assured Kate that the situation would be resolved.

Meanwhile, Ashton finally confessed that he was confused by his sexuality, but assured Kate that he loved her. She found this hard to believe, since he acted as though she didn't exist. The couple barely spoke, and he showed no interested in anything Kate had to say.

In fact, Ashton was starting to become emotionally abusive to Kate and began calling her names and ridiculing her appearance. When she told him that she was considering a divorce, he got physically aggressive with her. The talk of divorce hit a nerve with him because the will stated that Ashton would need to stay married for at least three years or he would have to return the rest of the money.

Kate told Ashton that she knew she had been deceived and knew all along that he was gay. Ashton told her that if she revealed his secret to the executor of the will, he would take revenge on her. "I'm not afraid of you, Ashton," Kate said.

"Well you should be," he replied. "If you divorce me, you'll be penniless, just like you were when I met you," he said. "I won't give you a divorce, even if you file for one," Ashton continued.

Kate made friends with some of the regulars at the nightclub in Florida where she caught Ashton with his male lover. They told her that Ashton and his lover have been together for a long time, and rumor had it, that he purchased a home for him and that he was providing him with a lavish lifestyle from the money he received from his uncle's will.

While this entire ordeal was taking a toll on Kate, it was starting to affect Ashton as well. He was squandering away money like it was water, had no interest in anything and even stopped taking care of his hygiene needs. In fact, he didn't shower or shave for days and wore the same dirty clothes for weeks on end. In a strange sort of way, Kate felt sorry for him.

Kate eventually heard from Blaine, the executor of the uncle's will, and was told that all the money that Ashton received when his uncle died would be taken back and dispersed among a variety of charities. Kate was ecstatic.

As soon as she heard the news, she packed up her belongings and moved back home to be with her family. She was worried that the estate would take back the home she bought for her parents when she married

Ashton, but Blaine told her that he felt that Ashton's uncle would have wanted her parents to keep it.

After Blaine contacted Ashton to tell him that he wouldn't be able to keep the money, Ashton went into a rage. He blamed Kate, but knew deep down that it was his own fault. He used her for his own gain, and in the process, he hurt a lot of people. His lover even dumped him, which further exacerbated his depression. This ordeal forced Ashton to examine his life. He came to the realization that people's feelings are more important than material things, and that as long as he was honest and hard-working, his life would be fulfilled.

Ashton tried contacting Kate after a couple years to apologize, but was unable to get a hold of her. Rumor has it that she started seeing an old highschool sweetheart to whom she is now engaged. While her current beau isn't rich, he is honest, hardworking and loving. The couple often talks about Kate's past life with Ashton, but that life is now becoming a distant, vague memory, as Kate is busy making happy memories with her new love.

****

About the Author

J.L. Ryan is a bestselling author who has written over 50 books, including the wildly popular Billionaire Boys Club, Billionaire Games, Billionaire Bachelors, and Adventures In Romance. Ryan has also attended numerous book signings and writer's conventions including Romance Writers Of America Conferences. Living in New York, J.L. enjoys spending time with family and friends, volunteering at a large metropolitan homeless shelter, and working in the dog rescue community.